Me and Rupert Goody

Me and Rupert Goody

BARBARA O'CONNOR

SCHOLASTIC INC.

New York Toronto London Auckland Sydney
Mexico City New Delhi Hong Kong Buenos Aires

Special thanks to my editors, Frances Foster and Elizabeth Mikesell; my agent, Barbara Markowitz; Janet Zade, who keeps my school visits running smoothly; my two favorite boys, Willy and Grady; my Duxbury writers' group; my good friend Nancy the Pool Girl Farrelly; and the Cherokee, North Carolina, Visitors' Center.

ISBN 0-439-39003-6

12 11 10 9 8 7 6 5 4 3   5 6 7/0

Printed in the U.S.A.   40

First Scholastic printing, January 2002

Designed by Rebecca A. Smith

For my dad, who sang "Sweet Jennalee" in the Smoky Mountains

Me and Rupert Goody

One

Before Rupert Goody waltzed hisself into Claytonville, I nearly always knew how my days would start and how they'd end. Could've bet my last nickel on nearly everything in between. That's how I like things—predictable. That's how come I spend my days at Uncle Beau's.

Let me explain right off the bat that Uncle Beau ain't really my uncle. Ain't no relation to me at all. Everybody in Claytonville calls him Uncle Beau. Always have, far as I know. Uncle Beau's General Store's been around as long as Claytonville has, I reckon. Maybe longer. Anybody looking to find me might as well start at Uncle Beau's cause there ain't no other place I'm likely to be excepting school. It's for darn sure I ain't going to be at home.

It beats me how come the Good Lord plunked me down in the middle of a family like mine—all wild and unpredictable. My brothers are all the time saying the reason our family is named Helton is cause there's always a ton of hell going on. Mama slaps them silly when they say that, leaving her red handprint on their cheeks. They start howling and holding their faces and she says, "Y'all hush up that bawlin' before I give you something to bawl about." Nine times out of ten at least one of them puts her to the test. "I swear, John Elliott, I'm gonna blister your hide," she yells. Then she's swatting and everybody's ducking and carrying on and I'm hightailing it over to Uncle Beau's.

When I complain about my ton-of-hell house, Uncle Beau listens and nods his head and most likely he'll say, "Well, I reckon that calls for a PayDay." Then he grabs a candy bar off the shelf and tosses it my way. I wolf down that sweet and salty treat real fast cause that's what I'm used to, eating the good stuff fast before somebody grabs it.

Uncle Beau always shakes his head and says, "Jeekers, Jennalee, slow down." But he don't have to worry about nobody grabbing food off his plate. Sometimes I peek into his little room back of the store. See all his stuff in there just the way he likes it. Nobody using his comb or getting dirt on his pillow.

Sometimes I pretend like I live there with Uncle Beau. Like I got my own little room back of the store. Got my stuff right out on the dresser and don't nobody take it. Even got my own bed. My ton-of-hell house is so filled up with kids that if I don't grab the daybed behind the kitchen, I get stuck with a creaky old cot or a lumpy bed that smells like pee, thanks to my sister Ruth. Imagine that. An eleven-year-old sleeping with a bed-wettin' baby.

Only way to get that daybed is to go to bed real early, which I do. That's how come I get up with the chickens. And that's how come I got to know Uncle Beau so good. He gets up with the chickens, too. Turns that sign around in the store window so it says, "Open." Puts the bargain table out on the porch. Starts the coffee to brewing.

Most of the time, it's still dark when I head out for the store. I ain't even to the front door good before I hear ole Jake's tail thump-thumping on the wooden floor.

"That you, Jennalee?" Uncle Beau calls through the screen door.

"No, it's Gravel Gertie," I say, which sets Uncle Beau to laughing. I got no idea who Gravel Gertie is, but Uncle Beau says she used to be in the funny papers.

I help Uncle Beau put out the doughnuts, trying not to lick my fingers cause he hates it when I do that.

"You gonna give everybody cooties, Jennalee," he says. "Then where would I be? No customers coming in my store giving me money cause they all home sick with the cootie fever."

When the sun starts peeking over the mountains, Howard Harvey brings the newspapers and some bushel baskets of produce. He takes the shriveled-up squash and rotten tomatoes to feed his hogs and I help Uncle Beau sort out the fresh stuff. I act like I don't know what time it is.

"Okay, Jennalee," Uncle Beau says. "Time to get that head of yours filled up with something besides nonsense."

"Shoot," I say. "Ain't nothing at that school worth my time."

Uncle Beau tries to hide his smile, but I see it. His eyes crinkle up and his whiskery chin quivers. He points his finger at me and says, "Don't you go gettin' too big for your britches." His fingers are all crooked with arthritis and sometimes I stare at them. Uncle Beau says they're "whomper-jawed" and cusses about them. "You get old, Jennalee," he says, "your fingers get all whomper-jawed and it's a damn hateful thing."

I go on off to school to waste my time till three o'clock and then I go right back to Uncle Beau's store. By then, there's folks sitting around on the porch smoking and drinking soda. Ole Jake looks like he ain't moved a muscle since I been gone, but his tail starts thumping again when he sees me.

"Want me to empty the bottle caps?" I ask Uncle Beau.

"That'd be good, Jennalee," he says.

I take the key off the hook by the door and open up the soda machine. Uncle Beau likes bottles, not cans. "Tastes better in a bottle," he says. I agree.

I empty all the bottle caps into a milk carton. I take the milk carton around back to the shed. Then I go back and sit on the front steps and listen to the grownups talk. Making jokes I hardly ever get. Telling the same stories over again for about the umpteenth time. Once in a blue moon a car pulls in, sending dust flying and making everybody stop talking and look up. If it ain't somebody from Claytonville, it's most likely some tourist asking directions to Cherokee, where the Indian reservation is. We stare, inspecting their car, eyeing their clothes. If there's a kid in the car, I set my face hard and stick my chin up, acting like this is my store. Somebody on the porch always says, "Just keep headin' that way and you can't miss it." As the car's pulling away, Uncle Beau'll holler, "Hold on to your wallet when you get there, Paleface." We all laugh.

Cherokee attracts tourists like a horse attracts flies. The streets are lined with shops and motels and diners. The Tomahawk Inn. Big Chief's Café. Running Wolf's Souvenir and Gift Shop. For five dollars, you can have your picture taken with a real Cherokee Indian chief. For twenty dollars, you can buy genuine deerskin moccasins.

"Made in China," Uncle Beau points out, showing me the bottom of the moccasins in his store. "All that Indian bullcrap stuff is made in China." Uncle Beau's got a sign in the store window says, "Why Pay Cherokee Prices? Buy Your Genuine Indian Souvenirs Here." He's got beaded belts and headdresses with colored feathers. Tom-tom drums and tepee salt-and-pepper shakers and wooden napkin holders with "Great Smoky Mountains, Home of the Cherokee" carved on them.

I love that stuff. I wipe the dust off, try on the moccasins, beat the drums. Uncle Beau don't sell much of it. I guess most folks would rather pay more to get their souvenirs from real Cherokee Indians. Sometimes they ask Uncle Beau if he's Cherokee. I know for a fact Uncle Beau ain't got one drop of Cherokee blood in him. "One hundred per-cent pure North Carolina paleface," he tells me. Course, that ain't what he tells them tourists when they ask if he's Cherokee. "Son of a chief," he tells them. After they leave, he looks at me and says, "Chief fry cook and bottle washer."

At closing time, I help Uncle Beau bring in the bargain table. I turn the sign around. Closed. Uncle Beau tells me, "Button the door, Jennalee." That means lock up. I eat a doughnut and give one to Jake. Uncle Beau opens the cash register and puts the money in a leather pouch. I do my homework while Uncle Beau listens to the news on TV. He only listens, cause the picture's all scribbly. Besides, he don't see too good anyhow.

Then I say, "What time is it, Jake?" Thump-thump goes that tail.

"Quittin' time," I say.

Me, Jake, and Uncle Beau walk along the road. I have to try hard to walk slow. Uncle Beau breathes loud and wheezy and he don't talk much. There ain't much to look at along the way except trees and honeysuckle. Maybe some blackberries. Sometimes I find things beside the road, like whiskey bottles or hubcaps. Once I found a burlap bag with a squirrel's tail inside. Uncle Beau nailed it to the shed behind the store and it's still there.

If it's warm, we might go down to the creek. Uncle Beau takes off his shoes and puts his feet in the icy mountain water. He says it's good for his corns. I jump from rock to rock and hardly ever fall in.

When we get to Mountain Creek Baptist Church, I say bye and head on down Arrowhead Road toward my house, hoping my sister Marny ain't got the good bed yet. I turn and watch Uncle Beau shuffling down the road, Jake ambling along beside him, sniffing at everything in sight and lifting his leg about a million times.

And there you have it, a day in the life of Jennalee Helton. Least, that was a day in the life of Jennalee Helton before Rupert Goody waltzed into Claytonville and upset the applecart.

Two

The day Rupert Goody came to town, me and Uncle Beau had oatmeal for supper. Funny how you remember little things like that when something out of the ordinary happens. And it was for sure out of the ordinary when the skinniest black man I ever saw walked into the store, looked at Uncle Beau, and said, "I'm your son, Rupert B. Goody." Talk about unpredictable!

I looked at Uncle Beau and Uncle Beau looked at me. Jake growled real low in his throat, fur all standing up on his back.

The man grinned at us and said, "That oatmeal sure smells good."

He looked like he could probably use some oatmeal, but I didn't say nothing. I just stared, too dumbstruck to think straight.

Then Uncle Beau, he staggered over to the couch back of the store and sat down, rocking back and forth and looking like he'd seen a ghost. His hands were shaking and his mouth was twitching and I just knew that any minute he was going to clutch his heart and keel over dead.

"Look what you done!" I hollered at Rupert Goody. "Get on out of here before I call the sheriff."

Rupert's eyes got big and he started jerking his head like he had a bug in his ear and grabbing at his grimy T-shirt.

"You deaf or something?" I stepped toward him. "I said get yourself on out of here."

Uncle Beau pointed his whomper-jawed finger at Rupert and said, "Wait." Then he held his shaking hand out to me. "Help me up, Jennalee."

He grabbed my arm and darn near pulled me down trying to get up.

He squinted at Rupert. "Where you from?"

"Fletcher, sir," Rupert said. "Other side of Asheville."

"He knows where Fletcher is," I said, moving a step closer to Rupert. I was delighted to see him move back a step.

"Who sent you here?" Uncle Beau asked.

Rupert stared at the floor. He was tall but he held himself like a little kid, all hunched over and shy-like. "Nobody," he said.

"What you doing here?" Uncle Beau looked Rupert up and down.

"Come to see my daddy."

Well, now, that was about all I could take. "Tell him to git, Uncle Beau," I said, throwing my arm in the direction of the door.

"Hold on now, Jennalee."

Uncle Beau's hands were still trembling and I could practically see the wheels turning in his head as he scrambled to think about this strange turn of events.

"You hungry?" Uncle Beau said to Rupert.

"I am." Rupert's long, skinny arms hung limp by his side. He darted a look at the oatmeal.

"All I got is oatmeal," Uncle Beau said. "You like oatmeal?"

"I do," Rupert said. "I like it fine."

"Then come on over here and have yourself some." Uncle Beau pushed his bowl of cold, half-eaten oatmeal along the counter. Rupert took one step forward and Jake growled. Rupert took one step back.

"Hush up, now, Jake," Uncle Beau said, real mean. Jake must have been as surprised as me by the tone of Uncle Beau's voice, cause he cocked his head, then slunk down to the floor and looked away.

Rupert put down the grocery sack he'd been carrying and commenced to eating Uncle Beau's oatmeal in slow motion, making nasty slurpy noises. Uncle Beau and I didn't say nothing. We just watched Rupert eat it all except for one little bite. Then he set the bowl down on the floor next to Jake. Jake looked up at Rupert, then over at Uncle Beau, then started licking that bowl so hard it wobbled clear across the floor.

Uncle Beau chuckled and Rupert grinned. I glared at the two of them.

"Jake can't eat oatmeal. It makes him puke," I said.

Rupert's grin drooped and he hung his head. Uncle Beau shot me a look that made me squirm a bit.

"Tell him he can go now, Uncle Beau," I said.

"I think me and Rupert need to talk awhile, Jennalee," Uncle Beau said.

I kept my feet planted on the floor.

"Why don't you run on home now," Uncle Beau said. If he hadn't been looking at me, I'd've never in a million years guessed he was talking to me.

"But we ain't emptied the bottle caps or brung in the bargain table," I said. "We ain't buttoned the door."

"Maybe Rupert can help me do them things," Uncle Beau said.

Rupert's head shot up. "I can do them things," he said.

I covered my mouth so Rupert couldn't see and leaned toward Uncle Beau. "He don't look like he could handle them bottle caps," I whispered.

Uncle Beau smiled. "Then I'll leave them for you, Jennalee," he said. "For tomorrow."

Well, he might as well have kicked me in the pants. Here he was, my only friend in all the world, throwing me out of his store in favor of a half-wit black man claiming to be the son of a one-hundred-percent pure North Carolina paleface. If I hadn't had such an ache in my gut, I would've been sure I was dreaming.

I couldn't get my legs to move. Then I felt Uncle Beau's

hand on my back pushing me. That's right—pushing me toward the door.

I looked at Rupert, all hunched over and smiling like he'd done something to be proud of. I looked at Jake, panting over that empty bowl. Then I looked at Uncle Beau. He made his eyes go soft and droopy and said, "Do like I tell you, Jennalee."

I shoved the screen door with both hands, sending it flying open with a bang. I stomped out of the store and across the road.

I found me a comfortable spot in the gully by the road and I sat myself down and watched the store till it got too dark to see. Then I got up and headed for home, not even caring if I slept in a pee-smelling bed.

Three

I walked along the road watching my feet. My sneakers were wet with dew. The morning mist still hovered over the ground like a cloud of smoke. Somewhere up in the trees a bobwhite called his own name out. "Bob White!" I tried to answer him but I couldn't do it nearly as good as my brother Vernon.

Just before I got to Uncle Beau's, I stopped. I was afraid to look up. Afraid that things had been so crazy and mixed up the day before that if I looked up, the store might be gone. But I did look up and the store was still there, same as ever. Still, I had a strong feeling that, inside, things were different. As I walked, I chanted to myself, "Please, Lord, let Rupert be gone. Please, Lord, let Rupert be gone."

When I got closer, I saw the "Open" sign and the bargain table. I heard Jake's tail thumping same as always. Then

Rupert Goody came around from behind the store, carrying a bucket, and I felt like somebody punched me right between the eyes.

When he saw me, he smiled and waved like I was his friend. Water sloshed over the sides of the bucket.

"What you doing here?" I said, mean as I could.

"Washing milk crates."

"What you washing milk crates for?"

"Uncle Beau told me to."

"He ain't your uncle."

I stood between him and the door and gave him my best glare, but it didn't seem to faze him a bit.

"How long you planning on staying?" I said.

Rupert lowered his head and looked down at the bucket in his hand. I leaned over and looked up into his face.

"You hear me?" I said.

He lifted his shoulders and let them fall back down. He had on the same grimy T-shirt as yesterday. Smelled like tuna fish.

"Is that you, Jennalee?" Uncle Beau called from inside the store.

"No, it's Gravel Gertie," I said real low through my clenched teeth. When I got inside, first thing I saw was the doughnuts already on the plate on the counter.

Uncle Beau looked at the doughnuts and back at me.

"Jake ain't had his yet," he said.

I dropped my backpack and sat on the bench by the

checkout counter. I looked down at my wet sneakers. Pulled my sock up. Licked my finger and wiped dirt off my knee.

"You and I need to talk, Jennalee," Uncle Beau said.

"About what?"

"About Rupert."

I could hear water splashing on the porch and Rupert making grunting noises. I kept my eyes on my feet.

"Rupert is my son, Jennalee."

I made myself look at Uncle Beau. He had those droopy-dog eyes of his. I watched him rubbing Jake behind the ears.

"What you talking about, Uncle Beau?" I said. "You talking about that black man out there on the porch?" As far as I was concerned, it didn't take a genius to see that Rupert Goody didn't have one little bit of Uncle Beau in him. Sure, Uncle Beau's name was Goody, too. Beauregarde Goody. But having the name Goody didn't mean nothing. Shoot, anybody could call theirselves Goody if they wanted to.

"I had a woman once," Uncle Beau said. "Sweetest woman this side of heaven."

"Aw, hell, Uncle Beau," I said. "I don't want to hear this." I set a bit of a smile on my face cause I knew Uncle Beau didn't like it when I cussed.

He pushed through the curtain that hung over the door to his room and disappeared inside. For one scary minute I thought he wasn't going to come back out. Thought that was the end of this conversation. But he came out holding a picture and handed it to me.

"This here is Hattie Baker," he said.

I looked at the wrinkled black-and-white picture. A young black woman in a sundress sat on a blanket in the shade. She held a bunch of wildflowers in one hand and smiled. No, more than smiled. Laughed. She was laughing and I swear I could almost hear her.

I studied everything about her. Her hair pulled back tight. A necklace of tiny pearls. No shoes. White socks with lace around the edges. Her skin dark and smooth.

I looked at Uncle Beau. He was staring off into space, still rubbing Jake's ears. I shook my head, trying to get my scrambled-up thoughts to fall into place. Uncle Beau and this Hattie woman was a bit more than I could digest.

I looked at the picture again. Hattie looked back at me. She wasn't pretty, but I have to admit she had a look of goodness to her. I tried to imagine Uncle Beau sitting on the blanket beside her. His arm around her. Handing her those flowers and maybe telling one of his corny jokes to make her laugh.

"So what happened to her?" I said.

"Just up and disappeared," Uncle Beau said. "Took my heart with her."

I never heard Uncle Beau talk such talk before and it was making my head spin. Why didn't he just hush up and go wait for Howard Harvey to bring the produce?

"I tried to find her." Uncle Beau stopped rubbing Jake

and scratched the whiskers on his chin. Jake put his head on the floor and sighed a big dog sigh. "I begged her kin to tell me where she went, but they wouldn't give me the time of day," he went on. Then he chuckled. "I didn't have no truck back then, so I drove my John Deere lawn mower clear over to Asheville looking for her. Took me nearly two days."

"You find her?" I asked.

Uncle Beau shook his head. "Never did."

"So what makes you think that man out there's your son?" I jerked my head toward the porch.

"Ever since Hattie left, I been waiting," Uncle Beau said. "Not waiting for Hattie. I knew she wasn't coming back. Didn't know what the hell I was waiting for. Just a feeling that left me thinking my life was all vines and no taters. You know what I mean?"

I squirmed on the bench and bounced my foot real fast. Jake jerked his head up and looked at me, then flopped back over on his side.

"Maybe," I said.

"Well, anyhow," Uncle Beau went on, "when Rupert walked in here, that waiting feeling oozed right on out of me and out the door."

I looked at Uncle Beau. His bushy eyebrows were drawn together, making him look a little too earnest for my taste at the moment.

"So you saying that you and me is just the vines and you and Rupert is the taters," I said.

Uncle Beau's eyebrows dropped and his body sort of sank. He put his hand on my knee and jiggled my leg. "You taters, too, Gravel Gertie," he said.

"Then where's Hattie?"

"Died."

My stomach did a flop. I watched Uncle Beau's face, hoping like anything he wasn't going to cry or something. But he just looked kind of dreamy-eyed. Being a curious person, I went on. "How'd she die?"

"I'm not too clear on that," Uncle Beau said. "Rupert said she must've took one look at him and keeled over from the ugly shock." Uncle Beau chuckled and shook his head. "The boy can make a joke, I'll give him that."

"He don't look like no boy to me," I said. "Looks like a full-grown man. Ought to at least know how his own mama died." I rubbed Jake's stomach with my foot. I could feel my face sagging with a frown.

"I figure I'll just take things slow," Uncle Beau said. "Plenty of time to fill in the particulars." He patted my knee and put his face in front of mine. He smelled like Old Spice. "That face of yours gets any longer, it's gonna hit the floor," he said.

I looked away. I knew he was smiling, but I didn't smile back.

"So," I said. "This Rupert person just waltzes in here and takes over the place. That right, Uncle Beau?" My stomach was churning up a storm by now. I kept bouncing my foot and trying to swallow the lump in my throat.

"That ain't right at all, Jennalee," Uncle Beau said. He leaned over and whispered, "You were right about them bottle caps. I should've done like I said I would and let you do 'em, cause he flubbed it all up. You take care of that after school, okay?"

I snatched my backpack off the floor and threw it over my shoulder. On my way out, I stopped and looked down at Rupert Goody washing milk crates on the porch. Dirty water sloshing all over everything. His fly was unzipped and he looked like an idiot.

"Barn door's open," I said.

But he didn't even know what I was talking about. Just kept washing milk crates like he didn't know he was messing up my life. Taking the only predictable thing I ever had and mixing the vines up with the taters.

I walked across the gravel parking lot. When I got to the road, I turned and looked back at the store. Rupert on the porch with his barn door open, sloshing water everywhere. I picked up a handful of gravel. Uncle Beau stepped out on the porch and waved at me. I threw the gravel at the ground and headed off to school.

Four

Now, when I got up in the morning, the day that lay ahead of me was a mystery. Some days, I got to Uncle Beau's and everything seemed like before. Produce to sort through, boxes to open. Other days, Rupert would be sitting there mixing up the apples with the tangerines. Forgetting to put the soda-machine key back on the hook by the door. Making me wonder what was gonna happen next.

After school, I'd sit on the porch and listen to the same old grownup nonsense as before. Only now, with Rupert hanging around, I could swear there was a tension in the air. Uncle Beau told everybody about his son, about Hattie's boy, patting Rupert on the back and grinning from ear to ear. I saw the raised eyebrows, but Uncle Beau never did.

Claytonville's so small you can't spit without hitting somebody. Everybody knows everything worth knowing about everybody else. Least, they thought they did till Rupert come. I wanted somebody to say, "What you talkin' about, Uncle Beau? That black man ain't no son of yours." But nobody did.

A couple of the old folks remembered Hattie. "You mean this here's Hattie's boy?" they'd say. Then they'd stare at Rupert and say, "Well, I'll be."

Some of the black folks give Rupert the once-over. Every now and then, one of them said something like, "Looks every bit of Baker, don't he?" But mostly they just give him the once-over.

I tried to put on an I-don't-give-a-hoot face, but the subject of Hattie Baker made me fidget a bit. Rupert, on the other hand, didn't bat an eye. Half the time he just sat there all glassy-eyed like he didn't understand a thing. Usually, he was caught up in some chore Uncle Beau had him doing. Rolling coins or checking the expiration date on the milk or something.

First couple of days, I'd find Rupert doing my jobs—the price stamping and shelf stocking and all. Ticked me off big-time.

"You trust him with them pickle jars?" I'd say to Uncle Beau. Or: "Don't know who can read them labels, the way he's put them canned tomatoes out there." I guess Uncle Beau knew how to take a hint, cause after a while Rupert was mostly doing other stuff. Stuff I didn't like doing anyways.

Uncle Beau got Rupert set up in the shed out back.

Wrote his name on the door with a black marker. "Rupert B. Goody" in Uncle Beau's wiggly writing. "B for Beauregarde," Rupert told me. "Same as Uncle Beau." I figured he was saying that just to get my goat, which it did, but I just said, "Yeah, right. Whatever."

I went in that shed one day while Rupert was picking up litter in the parking lot. Nothing but a dirty old sleeping bag on an air mattress. A couple of shirts hanging on nails. Cardboard box full of socks and overalls and stuff. When I recognized the grocery sack Rupert had brought with him that first day he come to Claytonville, I couldn't stop myself from looking inside. What I saw convinced me more than ever that Rupert was plumb off his rocker. A stack of Monopoly money in a rubber band, a box of Fig Newtons, some tiny knitted booties, shoe polish, rusty pliers, and a mayonnaise jar full of buttons and bird feathers. That was it. I was beginning to think maybe Rupert Goody'd escaped from the loony bin.

I thought about it awhile before I decided to bring the subject up to Uncle Beau. Finally one day I said, "So, Uncle Beau, what you think is wrong with Rupert anyways?"

Uncle Beau was sitting on his lumpy old couch by the magazine rack. Had a portable heater setting right smack in front of him going full blast. It was nearly June and didn't feel a bit cold to me, but Uncle Beau, he got cold a lot. He scratched his whiskers. "Just a mite slow, I reckon," he said.

"Slow?" I let out a little "Hmmmf" and shook my head.

Uncle Beau raised one eyebrow. "Speak your mind, Jennalee," he said in a tone I didn't much like.

"Seems a tad more than slow to me, is all," I said.

Uncle Beau looked at me for a bit too long before he spoke. "Sometimes what's in a heart means a hell of a lot more than what's in a head."

I jabbed at the floor with the toe of my sneaker. "Maybe he ain't really your son." There, I said it. I listened to the heater whirring and waited. I hoped Rupert didn't come barging in. Uncle Beau pushed hisself up off the couch with a grunt. He walked in that shuffling way of his to the front door and squinted out into the parking lot.

"Looks like that storm is headin' our way," he said.

That shut me up. I felt about as low as a slithery ole snake in the grass. Then, just as I was scrambling for a way to redeem myself, in came Rupert, waving a paint scraper in the air.

"That old paint come off the door real good, Uncle Beau," he said. Little flecks of green paint stuck to his face and arms.

"That's good," said Uncle Beau. "What color you think we ought to paint it now?"

Rupert looked at me. "What you think, Jennalee?"

I looked at Uncle Beau, but he wasn't doing nothing to help me feel any better. "Whatever," I said.

"I think I got some paint out in the shed," Uncle Beau said, disappearing out the door.

I looked at Rupert. He smiled at me and I set my frown even harder.

"I reckon your family over in Fletcher must be worried about you," I said.

Rupert shook his head and looked down at his hands, fiddling with the paint scraper.

"Ain't your family looking for you?"

Rupert shook his head again.

"Must be somebody looking for you." I peered into Rupert's face. "Who'd you live with before you come here?"

"All them people," Rupert said.

"What people?"

"Nana June and Miss Sophie and Mr. Reuben and Anna Lee and . . ."

"Who're they?"

"Them people I lived with."

I squinted harder at Rupert. "Them people you lived with where?"

"In the homes," he said.

"You mean the home? Like an orphanage?"

"He means the foster homes," Uncle Beau said behind me.

I jumped. "Oh," I said, feeling my face burning.

"Maybe we should head on over to Cherokee on Saturday," Uncle Beau said. Was he talking to me or Rupert? My stomach was nothing but a ball of knots till he added, "Must be about ruby-mine time, don't you reckon, Jennalee?"

I felt a smile spread across my face. Nothing I like better than going to the ruby mine with Uncle Beau. It ain't a real mine. They just call it that. They got these long troughs with water running through them. You buy yourself a bucket of dirt. Five dollars for a regular bucket. Eight for a giant-size. You put a scoop of dirt in a sieve and slosh the sieve around in the water till all the dirt is washed away and ain't nothing left in the sieve but rocks. Then you pick through them rocks and see if you got yourself a ruby. Course, it ain't a shiny red ruby like's in a ring or nothing. It's just a reddish-looking rock's got to be cut and polished. I been collecting rubies for years. Got me a whole bunch in a Whitman's candy box. My sister Marny's all the time telling me the ruby mine is a rip-off, that them rubies ain't worth nothing, but I know she'd love to get her grimy old hands on them if she could. Good news is she can't, cause I keep my box at Uncle Beau's.

So, anyway, when Uncle Beau said that about going to Cherokee, I felt my spirits lift. "Yeah, that'd be good," I said.

"You ever been ruby mining, Rupert?" Uncle Beau said.

Rupert ran his thumb over the paint scraper and stuck his tongue out of the corner of his mouth. He squinted his eyes up like he was thinking real hard about whether or not he'd ever been ruby mining. Way I saw it, either he had or he hadn't, but I kept quiet.

Finally, he looked at Uncle Beau and shook his head so hard his cheeks jiggled. "No, I ain't," he said.

"Well, now, that's okay," Uncle Beau said. "Jennalee's bout the best ruby miner in North Carolina. I bet she'd give you a tip or two if you asked her."

Rupert scratched at the paint flecks on his arm. "You help me, Jennalee?" he said. "You give me a tip or two?"

I shrugged. "I guess."

"Okay, then," Uncle Beau said. "That's what we'll do." He pulled his pocket watch out and flipped it open. "Hoooeee," he said. "Where'd this day go?"

"What time is it, Jake? Quittin' time," Rupert said. "Button the door, Jennalee."

Uncle Beau laughed so hard he had to sit back down on the couch.

"You beat all, Rupert," he said, wiping his eyes with a handkerchief. "Don't Rupert beat all, Jennalee?"

"Yeah," I said. "Rupert sure beats all."

Five

It was still dark when we left Claytonville and headed for Cherokee. I squeezed my knees together and leaned over next to the door of Uncle Beau's pickup so I wouldn't touch Rupert. The morning air was chilly and damp. I pulled the hood of my sweatshirt over my head and stuffed my hands in the pockets.

We chugged along the winding mountain roads in silence. That was fine with me. I like reading the signs along the way. Usually I read them out loud to Uncle Beau, but with Rupert beside me, I read them to myself. Mountainview Motel, Five Miles Ahead, TV, Pool, Air-Conditioned. My favorite signs are the ones announcing the souvenir shops. Big yellow signs, one after the other, letting folks know what was coming. Pecans. Honey. Boiled Peanuts. Indian Blankets.

By the time we got to Cherokee, the sun was up and the chill had left the air.

"My stomach's begging for some ham biscuits," Uncle Beau said. "Y'all hungry?"

"We going to Thelma's?" I asked. Me and Uncle Beau always eat at Thelma's. I always get the Big Chief Special. Uncle Beau gets ham biscuits and grits.

"Course we're going to Thelma's," Uncle Beau said. "Rupert, you wanna go to Thelma's?"

"Sure I do," Rupert said, nodding like he knew what the heck Thelma's was.

We sat at the counter and Thelma said, "Hey," giving ole Rupert the eye.

"This here's my son, Rupert," Uncle Beau said.

Thelma said, "That's nice," but I bet she was thinking something else.

"I want the greasiest ham biscuits you can scrounge up," Uncle Beau said. "And grits."

Thelma scribbled on a pad and then looked at me. "I'll have the Big Chief Special," I said.

She scribbled again and then looked at Rupert.

"Give him some ham biscuits, too," Uncle Beau said.

"I'll have the Big Chief Special," Rupert said.

"Why you have to go and copy me all the time, Rupert," I snapped.

He looked down at his hands, clutching and twisting his napkin. Doesn't take much to dull his shine, I thought to myself, trying hard as I could not to smile. Then I made the mistake of looking at Uncle Beau. He was looking at me and shaking his head, his eyes all hangdog and watery.

I didn't much enjoy my Big Chief Special that day.

By the time we got to the ruby mine, it was warm. A good day for mining. Uncle Beau backed the truck in so he and Jake could sit in the back and watch. Uncle Beau never did mine. Just liked to watch. Call out, "You get anything, Gravel Gertie?" craning his neck to see what I got.

Uncle Beau buys my buckets. I never did feel right taking money for the work I did in the store and he never did feel right letting me work for nothing. So we came to an agreement. Ruby mining. Two buckets. Ten dollars.

Course, I couldn't help but notice Rupert got two buckets, too. If I didn't know better, I'd've thought somebody died and left Uncle Beau a millionaire, the way he was buying them buckets that day. But I kept my mouth shut.

I set to work scooping and sieving and sorting through them rocks. Rupert sat next to me, watching every little thing I did and doing the same thing. I scooped. He scooped. I shook the sieve. He shook the sieve. I didn't let on, but it like to run me wild.

After a few scoops, I found myself a ruby.

"I got one!" I yelled, holding up a ruby about the size of a pea.

"I got one!" Rupert yelled, holding up a muddy ole piece of gravel.

"That ain't no ruby," I said.

31

He shrugged and looked kind of bumfuzzled. I put my ruby in a plastic bag and set to work scooping and sieving again.

Uncle Beau sat on the tailgate of the pickup, swinging his legs and scratching Jake. Every now and then, he called over to us, "How y'all doing?"

I'd hold up my bag and show the rubies I had. Not too many. Mostly little tiny ones. Rupert's bag had all kinds of rocks in it. Might have been a ruby or two in there, but I wasn't going to tell him.

Suddenly Rupert yelled, "I got one!" so loud it scared the bejeezus out of me. Made everyone in the ruby mine look at us. Rupert held up a rock big as a golf ball.

The man who works there came running over with his eyes wide and his mouth open.

"Lookee here, folks," he said, pointing to Rupert's ruby. "Look at the size of this ruby!" He held his hand out to Rupert. "Let me shake your hand, mister, cause today's your lucky day."

Rupert nearly pumped that guy's arm plumb off and held up the ruby for everyone to see.

Uncle Beau came over and took the ruby. Rolled it around in his hands. Held it up to the light. "Sure looks like a ruby," he said.

"That's cause it is a ruby," the man said. "That one's worth a bunch, that's for sure."

"How much?" Uncle Beau asked.

"Well, it's hard to say, lest it was cut." The man talked

real loud so everyone could hear. "But I know this, I ain't seen a ruby this big in a long time. Just goes to show, you buy enough buckets, you're bound to get a big one sooner or later."

"Well, now," Uncle Beau said. "Maybe we don't want to get it cut. How much is it worth then?"

"Ain't worth a milk bucket under a bull," the man said. "You got to get it cut."

"Where would we get it cut?"

"Right here, mister. Right here." The man took the ruby and examined it, then whistled and shook his head. "This here's a beauty, all right. Since I ain't seen one this nice before, I'll give you a deal. Eighteen hundred bucks."

Uncle Beau let out a "pffft" and waved his hand. "You must have me mixed up with a fool, mister," he said.

The man shrugged. "Have it your way. Lowest I could go is fifteen hundred. Ain't nobody in North Carolina'd cut that stone for less than that. I expect that ruby'd be worth five or six times that after it was cut."

I watched this scene with a growing feeling of upset. I'd been to this ruby mine about a billion times before, scooping and sieving for hours, and ain't never found a ruby come close to that one. Now along comes Rupert B. Goody, too dumb to know left from right or up from down, finds himself a ruby like that. I clenched my teeth real tight and shot Rupert a look.

I was almost hoping Marny was right. She was all the time telling me the ruby mine stayed in business thanks to fools like me. "You're so stupid I can't hardly believe it, Jennalee," she says to me. "Them rubies ain't worth nothing, cut or not. You think them crooks would be putting priceless rubies in a bucket of dirt? Get real, Jennalee."

Still, when I saw that big ruby in Rupert's hand, I couldn't stop myself from feeling eat up with jealous.

Uncle Beau patted Rupert on the back. "Well, I guess you got yourself something worth holding on to."

Rupert nodded and put the ruby in the pocket of his overalls.

The ride home was long and quiet. I watched the signs along the roadside go by, but I didn't read them. I was too stirred up inside to keep my mind on anything but Rupert Goody nosing his way into everything.

Uncle Beau tried to get a conversation going.

"Jennalee's got a whole boxful of rubies, don't you, Jennalee?" he said.

"Mmmm."

I could feel Rupert staring at me, but I kept my head turned toward the window.

"How many rubies you got, Jennalee?" Rupert said.

"A bunch."

"Big ones?"

"Nope."

"Little ones?"

"Yep."

"What you gonna do with all them rubies, Jennalee?"

"Make me a crown and call myself Queen of the World." There. That shut him up. I smiled at my reflection in the window.

We weren't even out of Cherokee before Rupert dropped his head back on the seat and started snoring to high heaven. Every curve we went around sent his head flopping my way and I had to nudge him with my shoulder. That's the last thing I needed was Rupert drooling on me.

Before it got too dark, I decided to take a look at my rubies. I took my plastic bag out of the glove box and dumped the dirty rubies out in my lap. Out plopped Rupert's ruby. There was no mistaking it, big as a golf ball, in the middle of my little pea-sized rubies. I picked it up and rolled it around in my hand.

I looked at Rupert, snoring away. Now, how do you suppose he managed to get his ruby in my bag? Just goes to show how sneaky he was. But I reckon the bigger question was, why'd he have to go and do a thing like that? I closed my fist over the ruby, feeling its roughness in my palm.

I reckon he thought he was going to whittle me down. Make me not care that he was horning in on me and Uncle Beau, taking the predictable out of things for me.

Rupert's head flopped over on me for about the hundredth time. I pushed it off me with my ruby fist but he didn't even wake up. I glared at him in the darkness, trying to send my thoughts his way. Rupert B. Goody, I thought, you trying to whittle me down, you might as well stop now, cause Jennalee Helton ain't one to be whittled.

Six

While Rupert was helping Ned Fuller put new shingles on his house, me and Uncle Beau drove over to Fletcher.

"I want to personally shake the hand of every person that's helped Rupert," he told me.

I didn't give him a chance to say whether or not he wanted me to go along. I just packed us some sandwiches and jumped in the truck next to Jake.

Uncle Beau had a list of names on a paper napkin.

"We'll just start at the top and work our way down," he said.

The ride there felt like the good ole days. I told Uncle Beau about how John Elliott threw a shoe at Jimmy and it busted out the window and a piece of glass flew clear across the room and cut Marny on the hand. She got about four itty-bitty stitches but you'd've thought she got her hand cut plumb off, the way she hollered.

Then I told him about how Daddy came home with roadkill and made a stew. I swear. The biggest rabbit I ever saw. Hardly a scratch on it. Daddy hung the skin on the fence out back and it smelled something awful, flies swarming all around it.

"Your daddy's a pretty resourceful man, ain't he?" Uncle Beau said.

"What's that mean?"

"Means he turns lemons into lemonade."

"I guess so. Only problem is, don't nobody want a thing to do with that roadkill stew."

Uncle Beau laughed and laughed. We ate our sandwiches and before long we were pulling into the parking lot of the Fletcher post office.

"Anybody works in a post office is likely to know everybody worth knowing," Uncle Beau explained.

He folded the napkin, put it in his pocket, walked up to the woman behind the counter, and said, "I'm looking for Miss Sophie Day."

"You're looking right at her," the woman said, without the slightest blink of curiosity.

"Well, I'll be doggone," Uncle Beau said. Then I guess he was so surprised to find Miss Sophie Day right off the bat that he didn't know what to say next.

Miss Sophie was about the tiniest woman I ever saw. Couldn't hardly see over the counter. She wore glasses thick as soda bottles. Her skin was as dark and cracked as old shoe leather.

"I know I ain't broke no law and ain't nobody died and

left me nothing," she said, "so what you want with me?" Then she smiled. If I had to count the teeth in her head, I reckon I could've stopped at about five.

Uncle Beau chuckled and held out his hand. "I just come to shake the hand of one who helped Rupert Goody."

Miss Sophie squinted at Uncle Beau. "Rupert Goody?" Then she looked up at the ceiling, rubbing her chin. "Rupert Goody. Rupert Goody."

Uncle Beau kept his hand out. "Tall, skinny black boy. A mite slow but sweet as can be. A good worker, too. Lost his mama as a baby. Floated all over Fletcher till he come my way."

Miss Sophie snapped her fingers. "I know who you mean now." She shook Uncle Beau's hand. "Lord, I hadn't seen that boy in ages. Last I heard, he was working for Mr. Reuben."

"Rupert's my son."

Miss Sophie's eyebrows shot up. "Your son?"

"Yes, ma'am."

"Well, I'll be." She looked Uncle Beau up and down, then glanced at me.

"This here's my friend Jennalee," Uncle Beau said.

Miss Sophie nodded. "Rupert stayed with me awhile when he was about thirteen, fourteen. I take in so many strays I can't remember one from the other half the time. I do remember Rupert, though. Couldn't read but could take my washing machine apart and put it back together. Not to fix it, mind you, but just for the hell of it."

Uncle Beau smiled at me. Such a proud, sweet smile I had to smile back.

"I never knew he had no kin, though," Miss Sophie said. "He was all the time saying he was gonna find his daddy someday, but they all say that. I never paid no mind to that kind of talk." She looked out at the truck. "You got Rupert with you?"

"He's back over in Claytonville working," Uncle Beau said.

"Y'all from Claytonville?"

"Yes, ma'am." Uncle Beau took the napkin out, smoothed it on the counter, and squinted down at the list. "Can you point us toward this Mr. Reuben?"

"I'll point you but I gotta warn you. That old geezer is about as mean as a hornet in a mason jar. Liable to run you off."

Uncle Beau tipped an imaginary hat. "Thanks for the warning," he said.

"Either you can't read or you're just stupid. Which is it?"

Me and Uncle Beau stopped.

"Neither," Uncle Beau said. "Just come to speak to you a minute, Mr. Reuben."

The old man jerked his head toward a sign. "Beware of Dog." I looked around. Wasn't no dog in sight. Then I heard the rattle of a chain and the ugliest dog I'd ever laid eyes on stuck his head out from under the front steps and growled at us. Mr. Reuben leaned toward us in his lawn chair.

"I don't see no lawn mower. That's what I do. Fix lawn mowers. You ain't got a lawn mower, then you got no business with me, mister."

Boy, Mr. Reuben would've made a good Helton. He'd've fit right in with them nasty brothers of mine. But Uncle Beau didn't let Mr. Reuben faze him a bit.

"Come to shake your hand, is all," Uncle Beau said. "Thank you for caring for Rupert Goody."

Mr. Reuben narrowed his eyes. "Rupert Goody?"

"Yessir."

"That no-good, sorry sack of nothing left me high and dry." Mr. Reuben threw his arm out toward his dirt patch of a yard, littered with lawn mowers and rototillers and greasy engine parts. "I give him a roof over his head and a good job and what does he do? Hightails it on out of here."

Uncle Beau and I looked at the yard. That ugly dog was still rattling his chain under the steps, but he didn't come out. Every now and then Jake let out a bark from the truck.

"Rupert's my son, Mr. Reuben," Uncle Beau said. "I just come to thank you for taking care of him."

Mr. Reuben cocked his head and glared at Uncle Beau. "Rupert Goody's a black man."

"Yessir, I know that."

Mr. Reuben grunted and waved his hand at Uncle Beau. "Go on, get out of here. I got work to do."

"You know anybody name of Anna Lee?"

"Dead."

"Dead?"

"That's how come Rupert come moping around here in the first place. Anna Lee died and left a passel of riffraff behind. Took in every kind of homeless no-account."

"Well, now, that's too bad," Uncle Beau said, taking out the napkin. "What about Nana June. You know her?"

Mr. Reuben snorted. "Over in that duplex by the Laundromat."

Once again Uncle Beau tipped his imaginary hat. "Much obliged, Mr. Reuben."

We hadn't been in Nana June's house fifteen minutes before I wanted to crawl in her lap and lay my head on her ample bosom. She was that kind of woman. Big and warm. All the time smiling and saying things that make a person feel like they was the most special person there ever was.

Her house was cluttered from wall to wall with toys and jackets and schoolbooks. Big, comfortable chairs and sofas were all squished together and just begging to be curled up on. The smell of something good baking in the kitchen set my mouth to watering the minute we walked in.

"Rupert Goody!" she squealed, taking Uncle Beau's hand in both of hers and pumping it up and down. "An angel on this earth, that boy. Come on over here and set yourselves down."

We pushed aside diapers and books and toys and sat on the couch. Nana June brought us homemade cookies and ginger ale. Two little kids peeked out at us from the kitchen.

"Rupert's my son," Uncle Beau said.

Nana June threw her arms up. "Law, you don't mean it!" She beamed at me and Uncle Beau. "You know, I've taken in nearly two hundred children over the last twenty years and I remember every one of them. And I do think Rupert Goody was the sweetest child I ever had the pleasure of knowing."

Uncle Beau grinned. "Did you know Rupert as a child?"

"Know him? Shoot, I changed his diapers and blew his nose and smacked his bottom a time or two." She patted me on the knee. "Is this sweet thing here your child, too?" she asked Uncle Beau.

"She's my friend."

"Well, now, ain't you lucky?" One of the kids in the kitchen peeked out again and Nana June held out her arms. "Come on in here, Luther." A little boy with a beach-towel cape ran in and buried his face in her lap. She laughed and patted his back. "Well, I'll tell you, Mr. Beauregarde, I love that Rupert Goody. I just can't keep no children too long. They stay with me long as they need to, then they move on. Rupert, he was kind of hard to find homes for on account of him being a little slow, you know. But I knew he'd find himself a home sooner or later. He was happy as a clam over at Anna Lee's, I can promise you that. God bless her soul." She shook her head and patted that little boy.

Uncle Beau stood up. "I won't be taking no more of your time. I thank you again for all you done."

Nana June hugged us both. "You tell Rupert to come see his Nana June."

"I'll do that." Uncle Beau started for the door, then turned, looking at his napkin. "You know either of these folks?"

Nana June looked at the napkin. "Well, let's see. Mrs. Singer went off to a nursing home over in Asheville. But that's been a ways back. I reckon she's probably passed on by now. The Stewarts, they left Fletcher about five years ago. I think they went up north somewheres, but I wouldn't swear to it."

Uncle Beau thanked her and we said our goodbyes, then headed on out to the truck. We were quiet on the way home, but that was good cause I had lots of thoughts. I thought about baby Rupert, sitting on Nana June's lap in his diapers. I thought about Rupert as a skinny teenager, helping Miss Sophie Day in the post office. Then I thought about grownup Rupert walking into Uncle Beau's store and saying, "I'm your son, Rupert B. Goody." I shook my head and gazed out the window at the darkening sky. Sure seemed like a puzzle to me.

Seven

I scooched down into the beanbag chair and stared at the
TV. Some man was shooting at some other man and some
woman was trying to run everybody down with a car. My
brothers were sprawled all over everywhere, watching that
show like it was the meaning of life. Now that school was
out for the summer, they spent their days watching TV
and hollering at each other.

Ruth came running in and they all started yelling for
her to get out of the way. She plopped down next to me.

"What you doing here, Jennalee?" she said.

"I live here."

"Why ain't you at Uncle Beau's?"

"I don't feel like it, okay?"

"I bet it's cause of that Rupert man."

"Shut up."

"Mama says he's Uncle Beau's son."

"Shut your mouth, Ruth Ann Helton!" I gave her hair a yank, but she kept going.

"I bet he is too Uncle Beau's son cause I seen him washing Uncle Beau's pickup and making deliveries to Miss June Tate and setting up the bargain table and . . ."

I yanked her hair again and she yelled, "Ma-a-a-ma!" Mama hollered something from the kitchen, and Ruth crawled up under the coffee table with her lower lip stuck out and her arms folded up against herself.

"You're mean, Jennalee," she said.

"You're stupid."

"Is that Rupert man really Uncle Beau's son?"

I put my hands over my ears and stared at the TV. Ruth crawled over and stuck her face in front of mine.

"Did Uncle Beau have a wife?" she said.

Now, that was just the kind of conversation my brothers had been pining for. They jumped right on it like a flea on a hound dog.

"Not a wife, Ruth," my oldest brother, Vernon, said. "More like a hot-to-trot girlfriend."

Vernon and John Elliott and Jimmy all started poking each other and carrying on like they were funny or something. I kept my hands over my ears and my eyes glued to the TV.

Ruth tried to pull my hands away. "How come Uncle Beau had a hot-to-trot girlfriend?" she said.

"Well, I reckon ole Uncle Beau is hot to trot hisself," Vernon said. He jumped up on the couch and started gyrating and carrying on. He hung his tongue out and panted like a dog and John Elliott and Jimmy rolled around on the couch laughing and holding their sides. Vernon was just pleased as punch. He wrapped his arms around an invisible woman and smooched his lips out, making kissy sounds. Then he poked the back of my head with his foot, but I just pretended like he didn't exist. Then I pulled my knee back and let go with a kick that sent Ruth clean under the coffee table. I realize I should've been kicking Vernon, but I wasn't no fool.

Ruth started bawling and they all started yelling for her to hush up and John Elliott started throwing pretzels and I got up and left that ton-of-hell house. I could hear Vernon calling after me, but I didn't stop.

I stomped off down the road, kicking rocks and soda cans and even a beer bottle or two. When I got to Uncle Beau's, I waited outside for a minute. Finally, I heard Jake's tail thumping. Good ole Jake.

Inside the store, it was dark and smelled like spaghetti. Uncle Beau pushed the curtain aside and came out of the back room.

"Well, hey there, Gravel Gertie," he said.

"Hey," I said. "You cooking spaghetti?"

"Burning's more like it. That damn hot plate's ready for the junkyard. Guess I'll have to settle for a loney-dog sandwich."

That's what Uncle Beau calls baloney. Loney dog.

"Where you been?" he said. "I was about to send out a posse."

I shrugged and ran my finger along the counter. I traced the dark brown circle stains left by coffee mugs. I wondered where Rupert was.

"You want me to stack them paper towels?" I said.

"Naw, Rupert's—"

"Okay," I said. "I was just asking."

In my head I said, "Where's Rupert?" but out loud I said, "Marny's got chicken pox. Fourteen years old with chicken pox." I laughed. "Sits on the bed looking in the mirror and crying all day."

"You take home some oatmeal," Uncle Beau said. "Oatmeal bath's good for the chicken-pox itch."

I flapped my hand in his direction. "Aw, let her itch."

Uncle Beau chuckled. That's what I love about Uncle Beau. You say something most grownups would have a conniption fit over and Uncle Beau, he just laughs.

I made my voice sound like I didn't really care when I asked, "Where's Rupert?"

"Over to Vernelle Aikens stacking wood."

I sat on the stool behind the counter and watched Uncle Beau ringing up groceries for folks. It was almost closing time when he said, "What is it about Rupert that's bothering you, Jennalee?"

I hadn't seen that one coming, that's for sure. I swung my legs and kicked the stool with my heels. Thu-thunk. Thu-thunk. "I don't know," I said. I kept my eyes on the floor, staring at a water stain from a leak in the roof, a coupon for $.35 off diapers, ants on a doughnut crumb. I heard Uncle Beau sigh. Out of the corner of my eye, I saw him rub his chin. For some reason, I wanted to say, "I love you, Uncle Beau." But, of course, I didn't.

"You been weighing on me, Jennalee," he said.

I looked up and wished I hadn't, cause he looked so sad.

"What you mean?" I asked.

"I mean I been seeing your looks and hearing your words and wondering where my Jennalee went and who's this little girl come and took her place."

Wasn't much I could say to that.

"Jennalee, you and Rupert Goody got a lot in common. You both like sorting the produce and you're both good at crazy eights and—"

"Me and Rupert Goody got nothing in common!" I hadn't meant for my voice to come out in such a holler.

"Why you so mad at Rupert?" Uncle Beau said.

I tried with all my might to keep my voice calm and steady. "I just wonder why he took his sweet time coming to find you, is all."

Uncle Beau lowered hisself slowly onto the couch. His knees cracked and his breath rattled in his chest. He rubbed his knees with his gnarly hands and looked up at me.

"There's a lot I don't know about that boy's life," he said. "May never know. Rupert ain't too smart. I realize that. But he's smart enough to know what family is."

48

"He wants family, he can have mine," I said under my breath.

"He belongs here with me, Jennalee."

"How come you so sure you all is family, Uncle Beau? You just going to take the word of anybody come prancing in here off the street calling theirselves a Goody? You ever ask him for proof?"

Uncle Beau took in a long, slow breath and let it out with a sigh. "Why don't you button the door, Gravel Gertie?" he said. "It's quittin' time."

I knew Uncle Beau was dodging an argument and I was glad. My head was all spinning around wanting to holler and fight about Rupert Goody trying to take my place. But my heart was telling me to slow down and love Uncle Beau, cause he was somebody worth loving.

Eight

I've never in my life heard of a grown man that can't ride a bicycle. As far as I was concerned, that was just one more item on my list of why Rupert Goody was crazy. When Sam Myers brought a rusty old bike over to the store and give it to Rupert, you'd've thought there was a carnival going on, the way everybody came by to watch. They all stood around the parking lot hooting and hollering while Rupert wobbled around trying to ride that bike.

"Keep pedaling! Keep pedaling!" they'd yell. Or: "That's it, Rupert! You got it now!"

But Rupert didn't have it. He'd squeeze his eyebrows together and stick his tongue out of the corner of his mouth and pedal so slow that bike would finally just tip right over and Rupert would lay there on the ground looking surprised. Then everybody'd be falling all over each other to get out there and help him up and dust him off.

One day Uncle Beau said, "Watch Jennalee do it, Rupert." He gave me a little push. "Go on and show him how, Jennalee."

Everybody chimed in, "Yeah, go on, Jennalee."

I took the bike from Rupert.

"Now watch, Rupert," Uncle Beau said. "Watch how Jennalee keeps pedaling."

Rupert nodded. "Okay, Uncle Beau."

I pedaled down the road a ways and then came back.

"See?" I said. "You got to keep pedaling or else you fall over, okay?"

"Okay, Jennalee."

"Now you try it." I handed over the bike.

Rupert climbed on. He looked like one of them circus bears, all hunched over on a little tiny bike. He started pedaling and wobbling and then he just fell right over in the gravel.

"Let's go on in and get us a Dr Pepper," Uncle Beau said.

Folks hung around for a while, drinking soda and talking. Before long, the store was empty and Uncle Beau went to the window and peered out at the darkening sky.

"Looks like we're gonna get a gully-washer," he said.

There was a low rumble of thunder, followed by a flash of lightning that lit up the sky. Uncle Beau and I went out on the porch to watch. We love a good storm.

Uncle Beau sat on the glider. It squeaked as he pushed it back and forth.

"Come on out here, Rupert," Uncle Beau called through the screen door.

The sky turned so dark it seemed like night.

"What's Rupert doing in there?" Uncle Beau asked me.

I looked through the door, but it was dark inside. "I don't know."

"Go on in there and see."

Inside, I squinted into the darkness, searching for Rupert. When I finally saw him, he was a sorry sight, standing in the corner with his arms all wrapped around hisself, staring at the wall and shaking to beat the band.

"What you doing, Rupert?" I said.

He didn't answer. Just kept his face to the wall.

"What's wrong with you?"

Still no answer.

Just then came a clap of thunder so loud it felt like the store was going to fall in on us. I thought Rupert was going to climb that wall. I could hear Uncle Beau out on the porch going "Hooo-eeee!"

"You scared of thunder?" I said to Rupert, moving a little closer.

He covered his ears with his hands and squeezed his eyes shut.

"Aw, Rupert," I said. "Ain't nothing to be scared of. Just noise, that's all."

Rupert wouldn't look at me. He shifted his weight from one foot to the other. Back and forth. Back and forth.

"Don't be a baby, Rupert," I said. "Look at Jake. He ain't even scared." But I wasn't too sure about that, seeing as how Jake was shaking pretty good, too.

Suddenly the rain started in one big swoop of a downpour. Rupert jerked around and looked toward the door all wild-eyed.

"My bike!" he hollered. "My bike!"

I followed his look and saw that beat-up old bike lying in the parking lot. The rain clattered down on it, making one wheel start to spin.

"Shoot, Rupert," I said. "That ole thing's seen more than a rainstorm, I can tell you that. Ain't no more places to rust on that piece of junk."

I turned back to look at Rupert and got a shock. He was crying. Tears rolling down his face. His chin all quivering. "My bike," he said again.

I looked at the bike, then back at Rupert, then back at the bike. I ran out into the parking lot, ducking my head as I splashed through the muddy puddles toward the bike. Just as I picked up the bike and started back toward the store, there was another clap of thunder, followed by a jagged bolt of lightning.

"Jennalee!" Rupert hollered real loud and awful-sounding.

Through the curtain of rain I could see Rupert on the porch.

"Jennalee!" he hollered again. Then he ran out into the rain with his arms stretched out in front. I figured he was gonna grab his bike, but he grabbed me in his skinny arms and like to squeezed the life out of me.

"Jennalee," he said.

I tried to pull away, but he had my arms pinned down to my sides.

"You gone crazy or something, Rupert?" I hollered.

When he finally let me go, I stepped away from him.

"Jeekers, Rupert," I said. "You trying to kill me or something?"

I turned to see what Uncle Beau thought of all this and my heart fell right to my feet. Uncle Beau was slumped over on the glider like he'd just up and gone to sleep. His whomper-jawed fingers were all curled up and his face was white and his lips were blue and it was for darn sure he wasn't sleeping. I'm here to tell you, that's a sight I'll never forget—but I wish like anything I could.

Nine

They said the lightning went right through that metal glider and into Uncle Beau.

"Damn near fried my gizzard," Uncle Beau said when I finally got up the nerve to go into his hospital room. I'd told myself, "Don't cry, Jennalee," about a hundred times, but when I walked into that dark, weird-smelling room and saw that wrinkly old man in the bed, the floodgates opened and I couldn't do nothing but cry. And then Uncle Beau said that about the fried gizzard and I just cried harder.

"Aw, come on now, Gravel Gertie," he said. "Come over here where I can see you. If I didn't know better, I'd think that was my Jennalee bawling over there."

"It is me, Uncle Beau," I managed to say. I hiccupped and sniffed and carried on, but I didn't care. This was some scary stuff.

"Don't cry, Jennalee," Uncle Beau said in such a soft, sweet voice I thought I'd die.

"You gonna be all right, ain't you, Uncle Beau?" I said, inching closer to his bed.

"Course I'm gonna be all right," he said. "Hell, that lightning just recharged my batteries, is all. Liable to make me better than I was before. Might've ruined my hairdo, though. Look at this." He ducked his head toward me. "Gave me chicken hair."

I wiped my eyes and looked closer. His white hair was sticking out every which way. I laughed. Chicken hair. That was a good one.

"When you coming home?" I said.

"Soon as I can find my clothes. You see my clothes anywhere around here?"

I looked around. The man in the bed next to Uncle Beau's was hooked up to about a million wires and was moaning. Gave me the willies. "No, sir, I don't," I said. "You want me to bring you something from home?"

"Maybe Rupert can do that."

Up until then, I'd forgotten all about Rupert. I hardly remembered calling 911. Seemed like a dream riding in the ambulance, holding Uncle Beau's curled-up hand and just daring anybody to pull me away. Rupert had flown right out of my head and disappeared—until then.

"What's the matter?" Uncle Beau said. "Something wrong with Rupert?"

"I guess I just forgot about him, is all."

Uncle Beau dropped his head back on the pillow and closed his eyes. My stomach did a flip.

"You okay, Uncle Beau?"

He breathed a few times real slow before answering. "Right as rain, Gravel Gertie," he said.

"I'll take care of the store, Uncle Beau. I can make the coffee and sort the produce and . . ."

"Naw, now, Jennalee," Uncle Beau said. "That store can wait. You just get Rupert to bring me some clothes."

"Yessir." I turned to go, just wanting to get out of there before my heart broke right in two from looking at him so old in that bed.

"One more thing, Gravel Gertie," he called after me. "You take care of Jake, okay?"

"Sure I will."

"And Rupert," he added. "You take care of Rupert, okay?"

I looked over at Uncle Beau, lying there so small and tired, his chicken hair sticking up all over his head and his bony arms limp by his side.

"Yessir," I said, and got out of there fast.

Back at the store, Curtis Rathman and Rob Sanders were waiting on customers. That kind of got my goat, but I guess they was just trying to help. I told them how Uncle Beau was and then asked about Rupert.

"He's locked hisself in that old shed back yonder and won't come out for nothing," Curtis said. "You better go check on him, Jennalee. He'll listen to you."

Just then my brother Vernon came busting in. "Jennalee, where you been?" he snapped, real bossy-like.

"Uncle Beau got struck by lightning," I said.

Vernon's face softened and he moved closer to me. For a minute I thought he was going to hug me, but then he looked down at my feet and said, "Damn."

"Like you care!" I hollered. Everything went all blurry through my tears and I blinked real hard.

Vernon ruffled my hair and jiggled my shoulder. "Aw, come on, Jennalee."

I slapped his hand away. "You don't know nothing about Uncle Beau," I said, throwing my arms out at Vernon. "For your information, he ain't hot to trot!"

I glared at him. The corners of his mouth twitched like he was trying not to smile, and I balled my fists up just in case he did. But he set a serious look on his face.

"You got to go on home," he said. "Mama's been looking for you all day."

"I can't," I said. "I got to look after the store."

"Me and Rob can take care of things here, Jennalee," Curtis said. "Besides, it's closing time anyhow."

"I got to bring in the bargain table and give Jake a dough-nut and button the door." I knew my voice was sounding a bit riled up. I tried to tone things down a bit. "Uncle Beau said he don't want nobody but me to mind the store." There. Nothing like a bold-faced lie to tone things down.

Curtis looked at Rob, who looked at Vernon, who looked at Curtis.

"You can't run the store by yourself, Jennalee," Vernon said.

"I can, too!" They didn't know nothing about the store. I was the one who did the pricing and emptied the bottle caps and dusted off the Indian souvenirs.

Vernon took my arm, but I jerked away. "Get on out of here!" I hollered.

Jake jumped up and trotted over, wagging his tail. He cocked his head and looked at me like I'd gone loco. Seeing his sad eyes made me remember Uncle Beau laying there in a hospital bed with chicken hair and I couldn't stop the tears from coming.

I sat on the couch and cried till I was plumb cried out. When I could finally look up and take stock of things around me, Curtis and Rob were gone and Vernon was trying to pull the bargain table through the door.

"Not like that!" I jumped up and showed him how to do it. "Vernon, I know how to do all this," I said. "Y'all just messing things up being here."

"You ain't running this store by yourself, Jennalee," Vernon said. "So you can help me do it or you can get your skinny butt on home."

I looked at Vernon and tried to read his face. I'd lived with him all my life, but half the time I never knew which way he was going to go. Like one of them eight balls you shake up and turn over. One shake might tell you, "Outlook good," but the very next one might say, "Don't count on it."

"Thanks, Vernon," I said.

He bustled around the store, slamming things and locking things and not looking my way. After we got the coffee urn washed out and set the squishy produce out on the porch, I said, "I got to get some things for Uncle Beau before I button the door. Then I'll be home."

I considered it a miracle when Vernon nodded and left. I looked around me in the silence. It felt kind of spooky. I was glad ole Jake was there, looking at me as if to say, "What now, Jennalee?"

I pushed aside the curtain and went into Uncle Beau's little room in back of the store. First thing, I got a whiff of Old Spice and felt the tears coming up again. I sat on Uncle Beau's bed and laid my head on his pillow. I pulled my knees up to my chest and hugged that pillow so tight it's a wonder the stuffing didn't come flying out. Then I had myself another good cry. One of those hiccupping kind of cries that didn't stop till I didn't have a tear left in me. What if Uncle Beau just up and died? What if I didn't have nowhere to be every day but my ton-of-hell house? What if I didn't have nobody to call me Gravel Gertie and give me PayDays and be my friend? I reckon I knew I was crying for me as much as I was crying for Uncle Beau, but I didn't care.

I turned over on my back, put my hands behind my head, and looked around Uncle Beau's room, my heart aching every time my eyes caught some piece of him. An army medal from World War II. His flannel nightshirt. A half-eaten piece of beef jerky. And then I saw her. Stuck in the frame of his dusty old mirror. Hattie Baker, sitting under that tree, holding them flowers. I got up and took down the picture. I stared at her, tracing her outline with my finger.

"I wish you could come on out of there and tell me the truth about Rupert," I said to Hattie.

But she just sat there laughing out at me.

I turned to Jake. He thumped his tail on the floor.

"Well, Jake," I said. "Let's you and me go find Rupert."

"Rupert," I called through the crack in the shed door.

No answer.

"Rupert," I called again.

Still no answer.

I pushed the door with my finger. It creaked open. I peered into the darkness.

"You in here, Rupert?" I stuck my head in and looked behind the door.

Rupert was standing in the corner, rocking back and forth, back and forth.

I stepped inside. "What you doing?"

If he heard me, he didn't let on.

I touched his shoulder. "Why you staying in here like this?" I said.

Still nothing. I pulled on his arm, trying to turn him around to face me, but it was like trying to move a cement post.

"Okay, fine," I said. "Stay in here, then. I'll just have to tell Uncle Beau you really are crazy." I started for the door.

He stopped rocking. "Uncle Beau," he said.

"You gonna come on out of this shed, or you staying in here for good?" I said.

"Uncle Beau's sick?" Rupert said. He turned and looked at me with his arms hanging down by his side and his shoulders drooping.

"Yeah," I said. "Uncle Beau's real sick."

"I made Uncle Beau sick?" Rupert whispered.

"Yeah, Rupert, you made Uncle Beau sick." I swear I couldn't stop those words from coming out of my mouth.

Rupert wailed the most mournful sound I ever heard. Then he started carrying on like I never seen in my life. He paced back and forth in that tiny shed. One side, then the other side. Arms flailing and head shaking. He rubbed his hands over his face and up and down his arms like he'd just walked through a spiderweb or something.

By then Jake was wondering what was up, so he came in and started acting kind of perky, like maybe this was some new kind of game we were playing. He even grabbed the leg of Rupert's pants, but Rupert didn't pay no mind. Just kept pacing and carrying on.

"I made Uncle Beau sick," he kept saying. "I made Uncle Beau sick."

Then, true to Rupert's unpredictable nature, he rushed out the door and took off running.

"Where you going?" I called after him. Jake started barking and I just stood there dumbfounded, watching Rupert disappear into the woods.

Ten

I laid on the daybed back of the kitchen and listened. The clock over the stove ticked. Low, garbled voices came from the TV in the living room. I heard my daddy come in the kitchen and open the refrigerator. He cussed when he hit his toe on a chair leg.

I squeezed my eyes shut and tried to make myself go to sleep instead of laying there listening—and thinking. Rupert was just crazy, that was all. It wasn't my fault he didn't have good sense. I wasn't the one made him act like a dang fool, was I? He was the one thought he made Uncle Beau sick, not me.

Gravel crunched in the driveway and headlights lit up the kitchen. Marny giggled out on the porch. She came in and shut the door real soft. I felt her looking over at me and I smiled to myself in the dark cause I knew she wanted my bed.

After a while everything got quiet except my daddy snoring in front of the bluish glow of the TV. When the rain started, my first thought was of Rupert in the woods. No matter how hard I tried, I couldn't stop thinking about that. The rain got harder, pelting down on the tin roof of the back porch. I tiptoed to the window and peered into the darkness outside.

Maybe Rupert wasn't in the woods anymore. Maybe a miracle happened and he got sense enough to go on back to the shed. I watched the rain in the light of the street-lamp by the road. Suddenly heat lightning lit up the sky like daylight. My stomach squeezed up and I closed my eyes and prayed, "Please don't let there be thunder. Please don't let there be thunder."

Then came the low, soft rumble of thunder, as if the Good Lord was saying, "Jennalee, you done a bad thing. Now suffer unto you the guilt." In my mind, clear as anything, I could see Rupert covering his ears and shaking like a cat in a roomful of rocking chairs.

I opened the back door and stepped onto the porch. The wind blew the rain, soaking my pajamas, but I didn't care. I squinted into the darkness, thinking maybe if I wished hard enough Rupert would be snoring away in his sleeping bag in the shed, dry and happy, instead of in the woods, wet and scared of thunder.

I didn't wait for the sun to come up. I hurried over to the store and ran around back to the shed. I could hear Jake barking inside the store and knew he was probably itching to get out, but I couldn't wait another minute to see if Rupert was in the shed.

He wasn't. It sounds funny to tell it now, but I actually went over and felt around on the sleeping bag just to make sure it was really empty. It was.

While I unlocked the door to the store, I could hear Jake whining on the other side.

"Hey, Jake," I said, patting his side. "It's me, Gravel Gertie." I tried to make my voice sound light and joking-like, but my insides were so heavy it's a wonder I could stay on my feet.

I knew Vernon would be mad at me for opening the store without him, but he was too slow for me. I'd already turned the sign, made the coffee, put out the doughnuts, and got the produce from Howard Harvey by the time Vernon got there.

"I told you to wait for me, Jennalee," he said.

I wanted to say something mean and nasty, but I knew it was because of Vernon that I was getting to run the store. I ain't no genius, but I know when to turn on the nasty and when to turn on the nice.

"I know it, Vernon," I said. "I just thought I'd get a jump on this stuff so you could relax a little before things get busy."

He gave me the eye but he didn't say nothing. Just poured hisself a cup of coffee.

"Where's Rupert?" he said, looking around.

I got the feather duster and started dusting the moccasins and stuff. Maybe he wouldn't ask again.

"Where's Rupert?" he asked again.

"I'm not sure."

"What does that mean?"

"I mean he ain't in the shed."

"Well, where is he?"

"I said I'm not sure." My tone was getting an edge of nasty to it. I cleared my throat and kept swishing the feather duster around on the tepee salt-and-pepper shakers.

"Where you think he went?" he asked me.

I shrugged, watching Jake sniffing at the doughnut plate. I felt my face burning hot and red, and I knew if I looked at Vernon, he'd see "I'm lying" written all over it. With that in mind, I didn't look at Vernon.

That afternoon, Curtis Rathman came by to mind the store and I went to the hospital to see Uncle Beau. His room was dark. I wanted to open the blinds and let the sun in, but I didn't. Uncle Beau was sleeping, breathing in and out real slow and raspy. I pulled up a chair and sat for a while, watching his whiskery face. He looked about a million years old. Every now and then, his mouth would twitch or his eyelids would flutter, but mostly he was still. I thought about him being dead. That was a terrible thought, I know, but I couldn't help it. I pictured him in a coffin, his chicken hair all slicked down and his whomper-jawed hands crossed over his chest. I imagined myself kissing his cold cheek. While I was thinking that terrible thought, my heart ached so bad and I felt so scared that I wiggled Uncle Beau's arm to wake him up.

His eyes popped open and he looked confused for a minute. Then he smiled. "Well, hey there, Gravel Gertie." He lifted his hand in a feeble wave.

"Hey," I said, worried that he might know I'd been imagining him dead.

"I hope you brung me some ham biscuits."

"Shoot." I stamped my foot. "I didn't think of it. You want me to go get you some?"

"Naw." He took a sip of water. His arm was all bruised, the skin hanging loose and wrinkled. I looked away.

"When you coming home?" I asked.

"Soon as that baby-faced doctor gets his butt in here maybe I can find out. I'd sure like to know what in the hell these damn doctors get paid for." He took another sip of water and dropped his head back on the pillow. "Did you tell Rupert to bring my clothes?"

There. I knew it was coming sooner or later.

"No, sir." I held up a paper bag. "I brought em."

"That's good." He took the paper bag and set it on the nightstand. "Is Rupert coming by?"

"I don't know." Well, I didn't know.

"He helping with the store?"

"No, sir."

Uncle Beau's eyebrows came together. "How come?"

The man in the other bed stirred a bit under the covers. "Shhh." I held my finger to my lips. "We better quiet down."

Uncle Beau flapped his hand at the other bed. "How come Rupert ain't helping with the store?"

"He's doing something else." Why couldn't I just make up a lie?

Uncle Beau squinted at me. "Like what?"

Then for once in my life the Good Lord was on my side. He sent in a nurse to rescue me.

"G-o-o-o-d afternoon," she sang, bustling around the room, opening blinds and plumping pillows. "How are we today, Mr. Goody?" She stuck a thermometer in Uncle Beau's mouth before he knew what hit him. I took that as a sign to get the heck out of there.

"I got to go help Vernon close the store," I said, making a beeline for the door. I hurried down the hall without looking back. Only one thing on my mind now. I had to find Rupert Goody.

Back at the store, Vernon let me close up by myself again. I did everything from turning the sign to buttoning the door. While Jake ate his doughnut, I made a cheese sandwich and put it in a plastic bag, then poured apple juice into a jar. I went around back to the edge of the woods and put the sandwich and the juice under a tree.

I stood for a minute looking into the woods, searching for a sign, listening for a sound. Then I turned and went home, dreading the thought of going to bed cause I had a strong feeling I wasn't going to sleep too good again that night.

Eleven

The sandwich and juice were gone. In their place were three little guinea-hen eggs. Uncle Beau's favorite. I squinted into the woods. Okay, Rupert Goody. Now you really got me messed up. I picked up the eggs and thought about throwing them as far into the woods as I could. Was I glad to know Rupert was still out there somewhere, or did I wish he'd've kept on going and never looked back? I don't know.

Me and Vernon minded the store for the next two days. Once in a while, someone would ask about Rupert and I'd toss my head toward the back of the store or flap my hand and say, "Oh, you know Rupert." That seemed to satisfy most everybody but Vernon. Even when things are smooth as ice, Vernon's like a lit firecracker. The sizzle before the bang. So I had to be careful when he said, "What you up to, Jennalee?"

I watched the guinea-hen eggs boiling on the hot plate.

"Boiling eggs for Uncle Beau," I said, trying my best to keep that firecracker from blowing.

"I mean with Rupert." He squeezed my arm, but I didn't let on that it hurt.

"I ain't up to nothing with Rupert."

"Then where is he?"

"He's okay, Vernon." I pulled my arm away but kept my voice calm. "I know what I'm doing. It ain't none of your business." I never should've said that.

"Well, I can make it my business." He pushed my shoulder so hard my head snapped back and my teeth clattered together. "Rupert's just up and disappeared. Don't that seem a little peculiar to you?" he said.

"Way I see it, Rupert's pretty peculiar hisself."

"You tell Uncle Beau Rupert's gone?"

The way Vernon was eyeing me, I was starting to squirm a bit. "Ain't no use getting Uncle Beau all riled up over nothing." I smiled at Vernon, but he didn't smile back.

"You've gone and done something, ain't you?" he said. "What you done?"

"I ain't done nothing." My voice got a little squeaky at the end.

"You know where Rupert is?"

"I got an idea," I said, shuffling my toe around on the dusty wooden floor.

"You mind telling me what that idea is?"

I could see that being sweet and reasonable wasn't working, so I switched tactics. "Yes, Mr. Bossy Butt, I do."

Big mistake. Vernon grabbed me by the shoulders and put his face in mine.

"I can call the sheriff out here. Get some hunting dogs out there in the woods to look for Rupert. That what you want?"

"Rupert's gonna come back, Vernon. He's just having a crazy spell, is all. Ain't no reason to go and get hysterical."

Vernon glared at me. Ordinarily, I could match that glare with one of my own, but that day I struggled to keep my face looking as close to sweet as I knew how.

"You listen to me now, Jennalee," he said. "If you've gone and done something stupid, I'll be the first in line to kick your butt. You hear me?"

I nodded and put the boiled eggs in a paper bag for Uncle Beau.

I'd had a small streak of good luck by timing my visits to the hospital just right. One time Uncle Beau was sleeping and once he was gone getting some kind of tests on his heart. But I knew it was only a matter of time before we met face-to-face and he said, "Tell me where Rupert is, Jennalee, and don't you go sugar-coating nothing cause I ain't in the mood." And that's almost exactly what he said.

"He run off into the woods back of the store." I peeled an egg and handed it to him. "But he's okay. I been putting food out for him. He left these eggs for you. I figure he'll be back by the time you get home."

I felt Uncle Beau's eyes on me, but I looked down at my

hands, busy peeling another egg. Then his thin hand covered mine, and I stopped peeling but I didn't look up.

"Why's he in the woods?" he said.

I forced myself to chuckle and said, "Well, no offense, Uncle Beau, but he ain't exactly working with a full deck, you know."

"You see him, Jennalee, you tell him I'm coming home and I need him to be there, okay?"

I nodded, squeezing my jaws together tight so my chin wouldn't quiver. I wanted to say, "Yessir, I'll tell him," but I couldn't say nothing.

The day Uncle Beau came home, Jake just about wagged hisself to death. Folks came by the store with tuna casseroles and sweet-potato pies and homemade pickles. Everybody fussed over Uncle Beau and told him not to lift that box or stack them jars, but he wouldn't have none of it.

"I ain't dead, you know," he'd say.

We all sat on the porch and listened to Uncle Beau tell about how he got his batteries recharged right there on the glider. Everybody laughed when he told about his chicken hair. Before long, it got dark and folks wandered on home. I could see Uncle Beau was wearing down.

"You want an extra pillow?" I asked him.

"No, that's okay."

"Might make you sleep better."

"I'll be okay."

"You want me to put a extra blanket on the bed?"

"I ain't sleeping in my bed."

"Where you sleeping?"

"I'm taking me a lounge chair out back and waiting for Rupert to stick his big toe out of them woods and then I'm gonna get him back in here where he belongs."

"Then I'm gonna stay back there, too."

"No, ma'am." Uncle Beau shook his head. "You get on home and let me take care of my doings my own self."

Well, he just might as well have shoved me off the porch cause I'd've felt the same way as I did, hearing that.

"They my doings, too," I said, hanging my head and feeling like a little bed-wettin' kid like Ruth. I lifted my eyes and looked at Uncle Beau. He looked smaller than I'd ever seen him look before. His shoulders slumped down and his hands rested on his bony knees. The quiet between us stretched out so long that ole Jake started thumping his tail on the floor like maybe something was up.

"Then go on in there and call your mama," Uncle Beau said, jerking his head toward the store.

I reckon it must have been about midnight when Jake jerked his head up and growled. Me and Uncle Beau like to jumped out of our skins, waking up from a sound sleep.

"What was that?" Uncle Beau said, sitting up.

I listened, squinting into the darkness. There was a snap, like a twig breaking, and the sound of breathing. Jake growled again.

"Hush up, Jake," Uncle Beau whispered.

Another snap.

"That you, Rupert?" Uncle Beau stood up. There was rustling and then silence. "You come on out of there, Rupert."

Jake trotted over to the edge of the woods, sniffing along the ground. Suddenly he stopped and wagged his tail.

Uncle Beau walked over to where Jake was at. The crunching gravel sounded loud and spooky in the dark. I pulled my blanket around me and shivered. Uncle Beau shined his flashlight into the woods. The circle of light darted through the trees like a lightning bug.

"I know you're in there, Rupert," Uncle Beau called out.

Silence.

"Come on, Rupert," Uncle Beau said. "I been missing you. I need you here with me."

Now, if that wouldn't break a person's heart, I don't know what would. The next thing I knew, Uncle Beau and Rupert were walking toward me, with Jake trotting after them.

"Let's go in and warm up," Uncle Beau said.

Even in summer, Smoky Mountain nights can be chilly. I was glad to get into the warmth of the store.

Inside, Uncle Beau turned on the lamp on the counter and I snuggled up in my blanket on the couch. Rupert was a mess. Clothes all dirty and wet. His shoes caked with mud. A stubble of beard on his face. He was skinny before, but now he was nothing but bones. And when my nose caught a whiff of him, I was hoping a bar of soap would be heading his way before long.

Uncle Beau sat on the stool by the counter and nodded toward the couch. "Why don't you sit down, Rupert?"

Rupert sat down and stared at his hands in his lap.

"Why you wanna go and stay in the woods like that?" Uncle Beau said real soft.

Rupert didn't say nothing. I pulled the blanket closer around me. I wished I could pull it over my head and disappear. Rupert was home. Why couldn't Uncle Beau just let it lie?

"How come you run off, Rupert?" he asked.

Rupert lifted his head like it was a sack of cement. "You mad at me?" he said.

"Mad?" Uncle Beau reached over and put a hand on Rupert's knee. "No, I ain't mad. Why would I want to go and be mad at you?"

"For making you sick."

"Now where in tarnation did you go and get yourself an idea like that?"

My insides squeezed up as I watched Rupert's face. His eyes met mine for about a half a second that at the time felt like an hour. Then he looked back down at his lap and shrugged.

Uncle Beau's eyes darted in my direction, then back at Rupert.

"It was the lightning made me sick," Uncle Beau said.

Rupert lifted his head and looked at Uncle Beau with his mouth hanging open. "The lightning?"

"Sure. Recharged my batteries. That's all."

Rupert stared at Uncle Beau for the longest time. Then he said, "Oh."

I pulled the blanket up under my chin and in my head begged Rupert not to look at me. I was already feeling about as low as a worm. If I got any lower, I was liable to sink right on into the ground. But Rupert did look at me. Too bad for me I didn't sink into the ground. Just stayed right there on the couch, a lowly ole worm wrapped in a blanket.

"The lightning," Rupert said, shaking his head in amazement.

Uncle Beau slapped Rupert's knee. "Now, what say we make some popcorn?" he said. "If I can get that gol-dern hot plate to work."

My stomach settled down some. That was just like Uncle Beau. Always knowing the right thing to say to set everybody at ease. Then, before I had a chance to pick my wormy self up and feel better, Uncle Beau put his arm on Rupert's shoulder and said, "Welcome home, son."

Funny how one little three-letter word can stab a heart right through.

Twelve

On the Fourth of July we cooked hot dogs on the grill out in the parking lot. Rupert ate four. We put marshmallows on coat hangers and roasted them over the hot coals. Rupert ate about a hundred. We tried to play horseshoes, but tourists in campers kept driving in, wanting ice or beer or hamburger buns. Uncle Beau would throw down his horseshoe and say, "Dang. Can't a body have a gol-dern holiday for one blessed day in his sorry ole life."

That night, Curtis Rathman came over with a truck full of kids and coolers and fireworks and Mrs. Rathman carrying potato salad. Rupert stayed in the shed and wouldn't even come out for sparklers. One of them kids kept saying, "Why won't Rupert come out of that shed?" and Uncle Beau kept saying, "Don't you be worrying about Rupert."

It was hot as all get-out, even when the sun went down

and the lightning bugs came out. I marched around the parking lot in my flip-flops, waving a sparkler in big figure eights. Used to be, Uncle Beau loved that. He'd sit on the porch and laugh. "You in a parade, Gravel Gertie?" he'd call out.

But that night he hardly paid attention at all. Seemed like he had his thoughts back there in the shed instead of out front with me.

"What does this spell, Uncle Beau?" I called out, waving and swooping my sparkler in the shape of letters.

Uncle Beau didn't even try to guess. Just shrugged his shoulders and smiled a sorry excuse for a smile. I was spelling my name, but I should've been spelling "Rupert Goody is an idiot."

Finally, I gave up and sat on the porch steps, hugging my knees.

"What's wrong with you, Uncle Beau?" I said, getting right to the point.

He looked kind of surprised for a minute, then he smiled and shook his head. "Oh, I don't know. I was just thinking about that boy back there. Wondering what goes on inside that head of his sometimes."

Well, I wanted to say, "Ain't nothing going on in that head far as I can see," but I didn't. Kept my mouth shut for once in my life.

When Curtis and everybody left, Rupert came out and we sat on the porch smacking mosquitoes and listening to firecrackers going off somewhere up the mountain.

"Why don't we take a walk on the wild side next week and go on over to Asheville?" Uncle Beau said.

I stared at him. "What for?"

"For my birthday."

I shook my head. "No way."

What was he talking about, going to Asheville for his birthday?

"Might be fun," Uncle Beau said. "I know where there's a trout farm. You can catch yourself a trout and they'll fry it up for you right there."

"But that ain't what we do on your birthday," I said. I could hear my voice starting to get whiny. Rupert was smacking his gum and getting on my nerves.

"I bet Rupert would get a kick out of trout fishing," Uncle Beau said.

"But what about the do-it-your-own-self store and the Sara Lee pound cake and the whiskey?" I protested.

Ever since I can remember, on Uncle Beau's birthday, he sits out on the porch and people who come to the store just wait on theirselves. Uncle Beau calls it a do-it-your-own-self store. He buys hisself a pint of Southern Comfort whiskey and sits out there rocking and talking and sipping out of that bottle the whole livelong day. Only day of the year I ever see him drink a drop of anything harder than apple cider. When the bakery truck comes, we get us a Sara Lee pound cake and I put candles on it, and that's what we've always done. I couldn't for the life of me see why Uncle Beau wanted to go and change things now.

I whirled around and looked at Rupert. "Rupert," I said, "which one you like better, fried trout or pound cake?"

Rupert looked at me and he looked at Uncle Beau and he looked back at me and then he even looked at Jake, who started wagging his tail like he was happy to be included.

"Pound cake," Rupert said.

Well, Uncle Beau started laughing so hard I thought he was going to fall out of his chair. Myself, I didn't see what was so funny.

Then Rupert started laughing, holding his stomach and rocking back and forth like he was a dern comedian or something.

Uncle Beau wiped his eyes and shook his head. "Rupert, I swear you beat all."

So on Uncle Beau's birthday I strung crepe-paper streamers around the porch and blew up balloons and tied a bow on Jake. I put up the sign I'd made four years ago: Uncle Beau's Do-It-Your-Own-Self Store.

A few folks came by to give Uncle Beau gifts. A load of firewood. An army knife. A crocheted afghan. I always feel bad that I can't buy Uncle Beau something nice, but he always makes a big to-do over the things I make. I'm all the time coming across some of the crappy ole things I made when I was little. A clay ashtray (he don't even smoke). A Popsicle-stick cabin. A crayon drawing of Jake (looks more like a dinosaur!).

Uncle Beau got out his pint of whiskey and sat out on the

glider. (I guess he wasn't worried about getting his gizzard fried again.) All day, he sipped and talked and even slept a little.

We had chili from a can for dinner and corn bread that Lurlene Macon sent over. Rupert tried to take the last piece, but Uncle Beau made us call heads or tails. (I won!)

After dinner, I gave Uncle Beau his present. Pot holders. He said they were the best pot holders he'd ever had. Perfect size. Nice colors. Sure needed them. Then I'll be danged if Rupert didn't go out to the shed and come back with something wrapped in newspaper.

"Now, what in the name of sweet Bessie Marie could this be?" Uncle Beau said, feeling all over the package. He held it up to his ear and gave it a shake.

"It's for you," Rupert said (like Uncle Beau didn't know that!).

Uncle Beau tore off the paper and what do you think it was? His hot plate!

"My hot plate," Uncle Beau said, looking as delighted as if he was holding a new fishing rod or something.

"I fixed it for you," Rupert said.

Uncle Beau's face turned all soft. "You fixed it?"

"So it won't get so hot no more."

Uncle Beau laughed. "Well, now, ain't that something? Where'd you ever learn how to do that?"

"At the lawn-mower shop."

"The lawn-mower shop?"

"One where I worked."

"You pretty good at fixing lawn mowers?"

"I can fix rototillers, too," Rupert said.

"Rototillers?" Uncle Beau's voice was starting to crack.

"And fans and toasters and hot plates." Rupert smiled.

Uncle Beau's eyes got watery and he blinked real hard. "Guess I never knew you could do all them things." He looked down at the hot plate in his lap. "Guess there's a lot of things I don't know about you."

The glider squeaked as Uncle Beau pushed it back and forth. We all sat there, looking at the hot plate and listening to that squeaking glider.

"Well, now," I said, jumping to my feet. "Time for pound cake!"

I brought out the cake with four candles on it. (That's as many as I could find.) Me and Rupert sang "Happy Birthday". Uncle Beau closed his eyes and blew out the candles.

"Did you make a wish?" I said.

And then it happened. Uncle Beau started crying. Not big boohoo crying. Just chin-quivering, eye-blinking, tear-rolling crying.

"Yeah, I made a wish," he said. "Wished I'd done things differently. Wished I could see Hattie Baker one more time. Wished I'd held Rupert in my arms when he was born."

Me and Rupert didn't move a muscle. Didn't make a sound.

"Wished Rupert could've known his mama," Uncle Beau went on. "Eyes like stars in the sky. A smile that could make a saint a sinner. Not that I was a saint, mind you." He leaned forward and winked at me and Rupert, making another tear roll down his whiskery face.

He took a sip out of the whiskey bottle and looked up at the sky. "Hattie, Hattie, Hattie," he said real slow, shaking his head. "I wish I could have just one more laugh with you, Hattie. Wish you could see your boy here, all grown up and fine as can be."

Rupert gazed up at the stars.

"That's all my wishes, Gravel Gertie," Uncle Beau said, leaning back and pushing the glider again.

Well, I knew this was whiskey talk. That's what Mama calls it. I'd heard it plenty of times from Daddy. Sad, weeping, loving-everybody kind of talk. "That's the whiskey talking," Mama always says, real disgusted-like. "I got no time for whiskey talk."

But coming from Uncle Beau, that whiskey talk sounded like coming-from-the-heart talk. I sat beside him and held his hand and helped him push the glider back and forth. Somewhere up on the mountain, an owl hooted. We all watched the sky, not talking. The stars seemed extra-shiny that night. The crickets chirped extra-loud. The breeze blew extra-soft. And I knew that Uncle Beau knew that Rupert knew that I knew—that Hattie Baker was out there somewhere watching us.

Thirteen

It took a while, but Rupert finally figured out which chores were mine and which chores were his. I didn't squawk about him putting the bargain table out, but he knew better than to touch the bottle caps or put out the doughnuts or sort the produce. We took turns dusting the Indian souvenirs. When it came time to stock the shelves, I let Rupert hand me the cans and boxes while I stacked them neatly, labels facing out. I showed him how to use the roll-on pricer, but half the time he'd get two or three price tags on one can and I'd have to peel off the extras.

Uncle Beau stayed busy with the summer tourists coming in and out all day. Sometimes he took a nap out on the porch and me and Rupert would mind the store. I wouldn't let Rupert use the cash register, but he was pretty good at bagging. At least he had sense enough not to put the bread on the bottom.

After supper, me and Rupert and Uncle Beau played Parcheesi on the porch till the mosquitoes came out. Then we'd go inside and watch TV and eat ice cream. Uncle Beau liked to say, "I scream, you scream, we all scream for ice cream." And every time Rupert would repeat it. "I scream, you scream, we all scream for ice cream."

After I turned the sign and buttoned the door, Rupert, Uncle Beau, and Jake would walk me home. Rupert liked to pull the leaves off the rhododendrons beside the road. He'd spread them out like a fan and wave them in my face. (That irritated the heck out of me.) When we got to Arrowhead Road, Rupert would say, "Adios, Jennalee." Every time. Don't ask me where he ever learned that, but that's what he said. Every time.

The end of July, I had to go to vacation Bible school at Mountain Creek Baptist Church. I've been going there since I was little, cause Mama makes us go there so she can visit her sister in Raleigh and know where we are till Daddy comes home. Now, except for Ruth and Jimmy, we were old enough to stay by ourselves, but Mama kept signing us up for vacation Bible school anyway. Vernon and Marny just flat don't go. John Elliott goes just so he can talk to girls. Me, I go for the arts and crafts.

The first day, I sat at a picnic table in the shade and used a strip of rawhide to sew up a leather wallet with a bear carved on one side and an Indian chief on the other. Imagine my surprise when I heard Rupert's voice say, "Hey, Jennalee."

There was Rupert, peeking out of the bushes.

"Rupert?" I said, even though I knew it was him.

"It's me. Rupert Goody."

"What you doing in there?"

"Nothing."

"You spying on me?"

"No."

"Then what you doing?"

"Nothing."

I looked around. I didn't especially want Rupert Goody at vacation Bible school. Groups of kids were scattered around the churchyard making lanyards and wallets or painting posters of Bible stories. Nobody seemed to notice Rupert.

"Get on home," I snarled into the bushes.

Rupert just stood there, staring at the wallet in my hand.

"What's wrong with you? I said get on home."

"What you doing?" he said.

"Making something. Now, go away."

"What you making?"

"This here's a wallet." I jabbed the air with the wallet. "What does it look like?"

Somebody's hand grabbed the wallet from me. I whirled around. Kevin Rochester and his gang of nitwit friends.

"What you doing, Jennalee?" Kevin said.

"None of your damn business."

"Who's that?" He pointed to Rupert, who ducked farther into the bushes.

"None of your damn business."

"What's he doing in there?"

"None of your damn business."

I heard Rupert rustling in the bushes. Why did he have to go messing up everything I do?

Kevin tossed my wallet on the picnic table. "I know who that is," he said. "I seen that retard over at Uncle Beau's."

To describe what happened in the next few minutes is going to be hard, cause it was a big jumble of craziness. I remember my fingernails digging into the palm of my hand when I made a fist. I remember the feel of Kevin's shirt button on my knuckles when I punched him in the stomach. And I remember Kevin's "oomph."

When Miss Gainer came running over all hysterical, I picked up my wallet, tossed my hair out of my eyes, and headed off down the road. I could hear her behind me, hollering, "You come back here, Jennalee Helton!" Kids were laughing and yelling and I didn't even look back.

By the time I got to Uncle Beau's, Rupert was sitting on the porch steps looking like a beat dog. I climbed the steps and looked down at him with my hands on my hips.

"You shouldn't've done that, Rupert Goody!" I hollered.

I stomped into the store and told Uncle Beau what happened.

"You're right, Jennalee," he said. "Rupert shouldn't've done that."

"He should've stayed where he belongs. What's he mean coming over there to church like that?"

Uncle Beau nodded. "He should've stayed put."

All this agreeing was making me madder. "You should've seen him, Uncle Beau. Hiding in the bushes, spying on me!"

Uncle Beau shook his head. "I don't know what got into him."

"I told you he was crazy!" I stamped my foot, then dropped onto the couch. I looked at my knuckles all red and scraped up. What had got into *Rupert*? What had got into *me,* was more like it. Why on this earth had I done what I done? Hauled off and hit Kevin Rochester right in the stomach in front of God and everybody. What did I care if he called Rupert a retard? Wasn't no business of mine. Maybe I was the one who was crazy.

That night we played Parcheesi in silence. I could feel Rupert's eyes on me, but every time I looked up, he looked away. Jake was having a doggy dream and whined and jerked in his sleep. Every now and then, somebody smacked a mosquito. When Uncle Beau said, "I scream, you scream, we all scream for ice cream," nobody said nothing.

I turned the sign and buttoned the door and we walked in single file down the side of the road. Jake, me, Uncle Beau, and Rupert. At Arrowhead Road, we stopped. I waited. Nothing. Uncle Beau pretended he was busy looking for ticks on Jake. Rupert shuffled a rock around with his toe. He looked at the rhododendron fan in his hand, then dropped it, watching the leathery leaves land on his shoe. I thrust my bear-and-Indian-chief wallet at Rupert.

"Here," I said. He looked at it, not moving. Uncle Beau nudged him with his elbow and Rupert took the wallet.

"Adios, Rupert," I said, turning and heading toward home. I was almost to my mailbox when I heard Rupert holler, "Adios, Jennalee."

Fourteen

And so the summer went. Me trying to keep things predictable and Rupert trying to mess things up. Leastways,
that's the way I saw it.

Like the time he come home with a cat. Mangiest-
looking alley cat I ever seen. Rupert claimed Hal Roper
give it to him for digging fence holes. Well, first off, if that
was true, then he got taken for a fool. And second off, we
didn't want no cats around the store. Uncle Beau is aller-
gic to the dern things, and Jake, well, you can imagine how
Jake reacted to the situation. First thing he did was chase
that cat around the store, knocking over stuff and sending
that thing clawing its way up the curtain in Uncle Beau's
room.

I figured Uncle Beau would make Rupert take that cat
back where it come from. I couldn't believe my ears when

Uncle Beau said, "You keep that thing outside, Rupert, you hear me?"

It wasn't two days before that cat was spending its days on Rupert's lap. Then, when it started catching mice and moles and stuff, Uncle Beau was just tickled pink. Me and Jake, though, we never did take a shine to that cat.

Then there was the time the dairy truck showed up at the store with a new driver. Never been to Uncle Beau's before. Me and Uncle Beau was busy inside, so Rupert, he decided to play Mr. Important and signed for the delivery. Even helped unload it. About fifty cases of yogurt and not one drop of milk. Well, trust me when I say there ain't too many yogurt eaters in Claytonville, North Carolina.

Me and Uncle Beau walked outside just as the dairy truck was disappearing down the road and there stood Rupert, grinning like he just saved the world.

"What in tarnation is this?" Uncle Beau said when he saw the yogurt.

Rupert looked at the cases stacked up there on the porch and scratched his head like it never occurred to him to wonder what was in them.

"They from the dairy man," he said.

So there we were with a mountain of yogurt in August (which, in case you didn't know it, is hot as blazes down here in the South) and nowhere to put it and nobody to buy it.

Now, if it was me, I'd've made Rupert pay dearly for that

act of sheer stupidity. But Uncle Beau, he just sit Rupert down and give him a talking-to in the nicest voice you ever heard. Rupert nodded like he understood, but I could tell he didn't.

By the time the dairy got another truck up the mountain, that yogurt wasn't worth eating, I can tell you that.

So things went along like that, all mixed up and crazy. And then came August 10, a day that will be forever etched in my mind.

We had played about a million games of crazy eights that day, keeping a tally of who won each game. (I was clearly the champion.) Right in the middle of a game, Uncle Beau had a hankering for pinto beans.

"Too hot for pinto beans," I said, waving a paper fan in front of my face.

Rupert had sweat running down the side of his face and every now and then he'd wipe it off, making the cards all dirty and sweaty and grossing me out.

"Aw, now, it ain't never too hot for pinto beans," Uncle Beau said. He set his cards down and went inside. I heard pots clanging and water running and then Uncle Beau came back out on the porch.

"There," he said. "Long and slow, that's the trick. Wish I had me a ham hock."

After we took in the bargain table, me and Rupert ate Popsicles on the porch steps. We had to eat fast cause they was melting, sending a stream of red juice running down our arms and dripping off our elbows. Rupert's fell off the stick onto the ground and Jake hightailed it over and ate it, dirt and all.

When the mosquitoes started coming out, I said, "What time is it, Jake?"

"Quittin' time," Rupert said.

We walked toward Arrowhead Road, Uncle Beau kind of wheezy and Jake with his tongue hanging out so far it like to dragged on the ground. Rupert kept stopping to pick stuff up off the ground. Bottle caps and shiny rocks. Even found an old sneaker. Uncle Beau walked so slow it didn't bother him none, but me and Jake, we had to keep stopping.

I turned and watched Rupert inspecting something in the weeds. "Come on, Rupert," I said. And then I saw it. Clouds of black, black smoke rising into the darkening sky.

"What's that?" I said, pointing.

We all three watched the smoke getting thicker and darker. Then the next thing I knew, Rupert was running. I never in my wildest dreams would have guessed he could run that fast, his skinny arms pumping and his huge feet barely touching the ground. Jake started barking and I turned and looked at Uncle Beau. The second our eyes met, I knew we both got the thought at the same time. The store! The store was on fire!

I took off after Rupert, but he was nowhere in sight. My heartbeat was pounding in my ears and I swear I could feel the blood racing through my body. When I got closer, I could see smoke rising thicker over the tops of the trees. Then I rounded the corner and saw the worst sight of my life. Uncle Beau's General Store, looking the same on the outside, but the inside glowing orange through the windows.

I stood in the parking lot, holding my hands over my ears to drown out the terrible crackle and roar of the fire. And then I remembered Rupert. I ran around to the side, yelling his name.

Then I saw him. Running out of the store with an armful of stuff that he dumped on the ground. Paper towels, cans of soup, bags of pretzels.

"Rupert," I yelled. "What are you doing?"

He didn't even look up. Just ran back into the store.

"Rupert!" My throat burned from the smoke, but I kept yelling.

When he came out again, I grabbed his arm, but he shook my hand away. He dropped more stuff on the ground. Toothpaste and shampoo. Rice and spaghetti. I tried to grab his shirt as he turned to run back in, but he was too fast. My eyes were burning and I could feel the heat of the fire on my face.

Then I heard Uncle Beau calling my name, calling Rupert's name. I turned. Uncle Beau was coming toward me, his arms stretched out and his eyes so filled with scared I had to look away.

"Jennalee!" he called in a voice I hardly knew.

We grabbed each other and held on for dear life. When Rupert came out again, Uncle Beau pulled away from me and tried to grab Rupert.

"Stop it, Rupert!" he yelled in a hoarse voice that I could barely hear over the noise of the fire.

Rupert didn't stop.

"P-l-e-a-s-e stop!" Uncle Beau hollered, his voice all hoarse and pitiful. Then he dropped to his knees beside the growing pile of stuff that Rupert kept hauling out of the store. He held his chest and coughed and I prayed with all my might that he wasn't going to up and die.

I ran to him and knelt beside him. All we could do was hold each other and watch Rupert. By then, he was covered with black soot, coughing like crazy, with a look on his face like he didn't see one thing but what he held in his arms. Boxes and bags and cans. Moccasins and tom-tom drums.

I could hear crashing inside the store and then I threw up. I wiped my face with my shirttail. Then I jumped up and ran at Rupert full steam ahead. I grabbed him around the waist and pushed with all my might. We hit the ground with a thud that took my breath away.

"Stop it, Rupert!" I screamed, shaking his shoulders so hard his head whipped back and forth. "Stop it," I said again, softer this time. His eyes finally met mine and for the first time I could tell he was really seeing me. "Stop it, Rupert," I said, giving him one more shake.

As soon as we got ourselves up off the ground, Uncle Beau come staggering over and pulled Rupert to him. I watched them there in the parking lot, in front of the burning store, beside that pathetic pile of groceries, holding each other and crying like I never heard nobody crying before in my life and hope to never hear again.

Then Uncle Beau held out his arm and motioned for me. I could barely get my feet to move, but somehow I managed to join their crying, hugging heap. I don't know how long we stood like that, clinging to each other, arms all tangled up and heads leaning together.

Then all of a sudden Rupert jerked his head up and looked toward the store. Before me or Uncle Beau could figure out what the heck he was doing, Rupert took off running toward the store again. By now, the flames were leaping out of the windows. Uncle Beau hollered for Rupert to stop, but he disappeared inside.

Uncle Beau said, "Rupert," real low under his breath, and started toward the store.

I took off after him. If he was going in there, then I was going in, too.

I thank the Good Lord to this day that, before we got to the porch, Rupert come out, coughing and sputtering. Uncle Beau grabbed the front of his shirt and shook like crazy.

"What the hell you doing, Rupert?" he hollered. "Get hold of yourself."

Rupert dropped to the ground and took big gulps of air. Then he held something up for Uncle Beau. Through my burning, tearing eyes I could tell it was that wrinkled picture of Hattie. Hattie Baker, smiling out at us from the cool shade of that tree.

And that was the exact moment that I knew it. Knew there was something powerful holding Uncle Beau and Rupert together. Knew Rupert had something in him behind that veil of crazy that Uncle Beau had seen all along. And as I watched Rupert that day, loving Uncle Beau like that, I knew that it was true. Me and Rupert Goody had a lot in common.

Fifteen

"But it ain't my turn!" Marny stamped her foot and glared at me.

"Hush up and do them dishes like I told you," Mama said, lighting a cigarette and blowing a stream of smoke up to the ceiling.

"She ain't never even here, Mama," Marny whined. "The only thing she does here is sleep. Why don't she just go on and move in with that old geezer and his retard helper or son or whatever the hell he is."

Mama did what I wanted to do. Slapped her silly. I figured I'd just sit back and enjoy the show. But then Mama whirled around and grabbed my shoulder with her birdclaw fingers and give me a shake. "What you grinning at? You get yourself in there and finish that laundry."

I didn't give Marny the satisfaction of looking her way as

I walked back to the washing machine. I put the wet T-shirts and jeans and underwear in the laundry basket and went out back to the clothesline.

I was nearly done when I heard my name.

"Jennalee!"

I looked up.

"Look at me, Jennalee!"

What do you think was coming toward me but Rupert Goody on a bicycle.

"Jennalee!" he called again. He stared at the ground with his eyebrows squeezed together, holding on to that bicycle so hard the veins were about to pop right out of his hands. Every now and then, the front wheel would start to wobbling and Rupert's smile would drop into a look of sheer panic.

He kept pedaling till he run right into the wet clothes and fell over into the dirt. He jumped up and brushed hisself off. "Did you see me on the bicycle, Jennalee?"

My smile came natural. I didn't even know it was coming till it came. When I felt myself smiling and saw my hand reach up to give Rupert a high five, I couldn't help but think about how quick things can change. Just last week, I'd've probably said, "Of course I seen you. You dern near run me over, you idiot!" But now here I was in my yard, picking up Rupert's bike and saying, "That was some real good bike riding, Rupert. I couldn't hardly believe my eyes."

"Uncle Beau's waitin' on the lumber man and then we can go," Rupert said.

Uncle Beau had decided that what we needed to do was

go ruby mining. "Ain't no reason to sit around whining like a bunch of crybabies," he had said. "A day over in Cherokee'll be just what the doctor ordered."

"But we ought to be here in case they do something we don't like," I protested. "What if they don't leave room for the produce stand or forget which side the dairy case is gonna go on?"

But Uncle Beau wouldn't listen. He wanted to go to Cherokee. Maybe it was breaking his heart as much as it was mine to see that pile of ashes that used to be the store. We'd poked around afterwards and found a few pitiful remnants of our lives before the fire. The blackened counter stool. A half-melted cashbox. The soda-machine key on a charred beam. But most everything else was a pile of ruin, except the porch, standing there all alone with the bargain table and the rocking chairs and the glider.

Uncle Beau had set up a cot back in Rupert's shed. Jake had wandered around the parking lot for a few days, then settled on a spot in the corner of the porch. Rupert's mangy cat run off for a while. Rupert stayed up half the night, calling, "Here, kitty, kitty," and leaving sardines out by the woods, till it finally came back.

The insurance company was going to pay for a new store. Me and Uncle Beau had made a solemn vow and promise never to tell Rupert that them men from the fire department said it was the hot plate caused the fire.

"I ain't eating another pinto bean as long as I live," Uncle Beau had said.

"Me neither," I said.

Now the construction guys were coming to start Uncle Beau's new store and my biggest worry was that they weren't gonna make it just the way it was before. But Uncle Beau said, "Don't worry, Gravel Gertie."

So off we went to Cherokee, me, Uncle Beau, Rupert, and Jake. I read the signs out loud and Rupert repeated everything.

"Rocky Creek Family Campground. Pets welcome."

"Rocky Creek Family Campground. Pets welcome."

"Smoky Joe's Gift Shop. Two miles ahead."

"Smoky Joe's Gift Shop. Two miles ahead."

"Oops! You missed it! Smoky Joe's Gift Shop ½ mile back."

"Oops! You missed it! Smoky Joe's Gift Shop ½ mile back."

When we got to Cherokee, we went straight to Thelma's. Me and Rupert got the Big Chief Special. Uncle Beau got grits and ham biscuits. When it came time to pay, Uncle Beau patted his pockets.

"Damn, I left my money out in the truck. Jennalee, run out there and look in the glove box."

I took a piece of bacon with me for Jake. I found Uncle Beau's money rolled up in a rubber band in the glove box. Beside it was Rupert's wallet. The bear-and-Indian-chief wallet.

Put that back, Jennalee, I told myself when I picked it up. That ain't yours, I said to myself when I opened it up. Stuff fell out onto the floor of the truck. I looked back at the diner, then picked up the things that had fallen. Rupert's things. A picture of a dog torn out of a magazine. A score card from Starland Miniature Golf. The Lord's Prayer printed in gold on a paper napkin. The last thing I picked up was a piece of paper so creased and worn it felt like cloth. I reckon that paper must've been folded and unfolded about a million times. I opened it carefully. And then my stomach dropped right down to my feet with a thud when I read that paper.

North Carolina State Board of Health. Certificate of Birth. Name at Birth: Rupert Beauregarde Goody. I skipped over the stuff about the hospital and the doctor and went on down to the part that said Mother's Maiden Name: Hattie Belle Baker. And then Father's Name: Beauregarde Samuel Goody.

My hands were shaking so bad I couldn't hardly fold that paper back up.

I didn't say nothing on the way to the ruby mine. When we got there, I got my bucket and scooped and sieved and thought.

"I'll be right back," I told Rupert. I hopped up on the back of the pickup next to Uncle Beau.

"Rupert's got a birth certificate," I whispered to Uncle Beau.

He rubbed Jake behind the ears and nodded. "I know."

I stared at him. "What you mean, you know?"

"I mean I know. I seen it."

"Where?"

"He showed it to me."

"When?"

"First day he come to Claytonville."

Well, now, I didn't know what to think about that. I stared down at my sneakers, thinking things over for a minute. A wave of mad come over me.

"You mean all this time you known how I was thinking that was a cockamamy story about him being your son and you had proof right there on a piece of paper but you didn't tell me?" I said.

Uncle Beau kept scratching Jake. He opened his mouth to say something but I butted in.

"How come?" I felt the tears coming and tried to blink them away.

Uncle Beau put his hand on my knee. "Cause you needed more than a little ole piece of paper, Jennalee." He squeezed my knee. "That piece of paper wouldn't've made you like Rupert any better. You had a wall built up too high, Gravel Gertie. Couldn't no piece of paper knock it down."

I let Uncle Beau's words sink in and settle down and I knew he was right. I should've said, "You're right, Uncle Beau," but I didn't. But I knew Uncle Beau didn't care about words. I put my hand on top of his and then Rupert called out, "I got one!"

All the way home Rupert kept sorting through his rubies. Counting them. Putting them in piles by size and color.

"What you gonna do with all them rubies?" I said.

Rupert, he didn't pause for one tiny little second. Looked me right in the eye and said, "Make me a crown and call myself Queen of the World."

Uncle Beau laughed so hard he had to pull the truck over to the side of the road. Rupert started poking me in the ribs, and the next thing you know, I'm laughing, too. The kind of laugh like I'd been needing for a long time.

"That sure cleans out the pipes, don't it?" Uncle Beau said, wiping his eyes and pulling back onto the highway. Me and Rupert nodded and we all settled into gazing at the sights along the way, feeling better about things and glad to be going home with our clean pipes.

The day the new store opened, I reckon nearly everyone in Claytonville came by. Even mean ole Marny came with John Elliott. Me and Rupert taped balloons up everywhere. Roy Mattson brought some of them triangle flags from his used-car lot and me and Vernon hung them up out in the parking lot. Somebody put up a "Grand Opening" sign like the ones they have in the big stores like Winn-Dixie.

We gave everybody a raffle ticket for a free turkey and Uncle Beau put dried beans in a fish bowl and gave a clock radio to the closest guess. (Nine hundred and thirty-five. I counted.)

We tried our best to make the new store feel right. Uncle Beau got a couch from the Salvation Army and Vernon and his friends brought it in and put it in the same spot as the old one. We put in a bench and a stool and even a calendar from Dixie Hardware and a lucky horseshoe over the door, just like before.

It was nice and clean and smelled good, but we all knew it was going to be a while before it felt like home. Uncle Beau said it just needed some life and that didn't come from a paint can, that come from living.

After folks went on home, me and Uncle Beau and Rupert set up the card table out on the porch. I think we took some comfort in being out there where things were old and used and familiar.

We played crazy eights till it was too dark to see. Then I sat on the steps with Rupert and listened to the squeak, squeak of the glider as Uncle Beau pushed it back and forth.

Before long, the squeaks stopped and Uncle Beau's chin dropped down on his chest and he started snoring that whistling kind of snore of his.

"What time is it, Jake?" Rupert said.

Thump-thump went that tail.

"Quittin' time," I said.

I stood up and looked at Uncle Beau, his cheeks puffing out with every snore, his whomper-jawed hands laying limp in his lap. Then I stretched and yawned and said, "Button the door, Rupert."